CHOSEN LIVES

MALA NAIDOO

Publisher: Mala Naidoo

website: malanaidoo.com

First published in Australia 2018

This edition published 2018

Cover design : WorkingType (www.workingtype.com.au)

Naidoo, Mala Chosen Lives

ISBN — 978-0-6481377-64

ABOUT THE AUTHOR

Mala Naidoo is an Australian author. She was born in South Africa during the apartheid era which is the impetus for her fictional stories that take on a life of their own when the creative muse beckons. Mala believes that literature speaks through the values and culture of characters' lives, situations, and choices, instilling understanding through connections to a moment in time, an event or conversation that brings clarity to daily existence.

www.malanaidoo.com

For My Daughter

*We must believe that we are gifted for something, and that this thing,
at whatever cost, must be attained.*

— Marie Curie (1867-1934)

1

DESTINATION UNKNOWN

Early on a Sunday morning, in late January, two eager women, unknown to each other, believed they were boarding a flight to Thailand. They were heading to the same mission that chose them for their outstanding contributions to society.

Patience spoke to her sister before she walked over to the departure lounge at the airport in Johannesburg.

'Go well, call me every night to let me know how you are. Promise.' Grace felt the pain of separation these past three months. Her sister's extended working holiday in South Africa, and now this mission in Thailand for another three months, left her lonely, she missed their heart-to-heart chats. They were yin and yang, gin and tonic to each other, honest and supportive in all their endeavours and life challenges.

'I will, just like I did from South Africa. I'm happy that Keefe is with you. Promise me you won't worry sis.'

'I'll try. Send lots of photos, you said the resort was stunning, so I want to see everything you're doing! Take care now.'

Patience hung up, leaving Grace unsettled about exactly what work-related project she was taking up in Thailand.

She had an hour before the flight departed, she settled down to read a novel she purchased at the airport bookstore. Claiming lost sleep was on her agenda, too, during the seventeen-hour flight. The last few days in Johannesburg were hectic, with many breakfast, lunch and dinner invitations, leaving her head in a swirl, and her body reeling from overeating. South Africans were known to be generous in feeding their guests with their favourite local dishes, and it was an insult to refuse anything on offer.

She was delighted to note there were no nagging or crying children waiting with flustered parents to board her flight. No howling babies to assault her eardrums! Blissful, undisturbed moments of reading, then a deep, dreamless sleep for at least six hours! The smile on her face was hard to conceal. She glowed with anticipation, promising herself that she was going to make the most of this new venture that came looking for her. Glancing around the cabin, she noted there were more women than men on this flight.

After five and a half hours of heavenly sleep she woke to join the line outside the toilet. She hated aircraft toilets, she felt suffocated, trapped when she was in there. The woman in front of her turned to her and smiled, opening up the opportunity for conversation.

'Great to have a quiet flight, with no howling children!'

'Yes, it was strangely calm, a bit too quiet for my liking. I come from a place with many noisy children. You don't have children around you at home?' the smiling woman asked.

Patience was pleased that the woman was friendly and keen to chat.

'No, my sister and I never married, so no children in our lives except for my darling dogs, Sprite and Ajax. I can't wait to see them again.'

'Are you on vacation?'

The woman introduced herself as Ming Xu from China.

'Nice to meet you, Ming, I'm Patience Sharvin. No, not a

holiday but it seems it could be one, I'm off to a training camp set up in Thailand. I'm a social worker and for some reason was head-hunted for this training. How about you?'

'Seems we may be heading to the same venue, I'm a school teacher and was also invited to an all-expenses paid training initiative in Thailand. I'm glad we've met. My community was suspicious about this offer, now at least I can tell them there is another lady heading the same way!' she laughed.

'That's great, I need a friend on this trip. My sister is such a worry wart, she too, will be pleased to know I've found someone going to the same location.'

They promised to find each other in Singapore when they landed, to get better acquainted en route to Thailand.

Patience was elated that Ming appeared calm and easy-going. She was concerned she might encounter some unfriendly, silent persons with no sense of humour. Feeling relaxed, she pulled on a pair of socks and settled down to read. Another nap was a good idea if she intended being fresh upon arrival. It would be a new life, for the next three months, and she had to be alert to what she had signed up for. She dared not tell Grace that she was unsure of precisely what was expected of her.

SHE ARRIVED IN BALMY, sticky midday heat in Singapore and marvelled at the surgical cleanliness and neatness around her. She dashed to the ladies' room to freshen up. Hordes of women came in to do the same, tidying up their appearance and smiling awkwardly at each other.

Ming waited for her at immigration clearance.

'Did you get some sleep before we landed?'

'Not really, I'm nervous about what I might have let myself in for. Three months is a long time.'

'It will pass quickly and soon we'll be heading back home saying just that.'

'Hopefully. I took a semester off from my teaching job for this offer.'

'I did too, although I run a shelter, or rather an organisation for women of domestic abuse. Now that I have trusted staff, I was able to get a break. I was in South Africa for three months.'

'Are you South African?'

'South African-Australian for the past twenty odd years now. How about you, were you holidaying there?'

'I had a few weeks before the trip to Thailand so I decided to get in a bit of South Africa. My uncle runs a business in Cape Town so I visited the family there.'

'That must have been good. I loved my time there too. Seeing my classmates from yesteryear was great. I'm chuffed that a safe house that has embraced the values of our Australian organisation has been set up in Johannesburg.'

'Wow, so your trip was really a working holiday then. I want to grab some sushi and noodles before we leave. I've never been to Thailand before so I don't know what the food is like there. I've heard it's amazing, but I'm a fussy eater.'

'I will be in heaven with the cuisine, it's my favourite!' Patience giggled, 'I should call to tell my sister that I've met the lovely you on the same journey, to put her at ease about my trip into the unknown!'

Grace was thrilled that her sister had struck up a friendship on her leap of faith adventure.

They heard the announcement for their flight, and hurried to the furthest end of the airport to a tucked away area for their special flight.

Queued up at the boarding lounge was a sea of women. Some familiar faces noticed earlier in the ladies' room nodded, acknowledging having seen each other before.

'This is like ladies' night at a clubhouse!' Patience squealed, 'now I'm really curious to know what mission we are on. I hope there are some gentlemen booked for this training. I need to have the company of men around, how about you Ming?' Patience laughed her deep husky, playful laugh, fascinated by the quiet crowd of women.

'I'm sure there will be a few men. I grew up in a female household so I don't particularly mind.'

'So did I, but come on, we need some men to balance the equation, you know!'

They shared a relaxed laugh, already at ease with each other. The age range of the women appeared to be from twenty through to fifty, or perhaps early sixties.

'Were you Skype interviewed for the offer?' Ming asked.

'Well, mine ended up being an email questionnaire because Skype was apparently malfunctioning on the day.'

'Really? I was interviewed by three women.'

'Soon all will be revealed, glad we are seated together on this leg of the trip.'

Patience looked around, feeling a little uneasy that she was not in control about what to expect in Thailand.

If it was going to be uncomfortable she sure as hell was not letting Grace know. The last thing she needed was Grace cavorting across the globe to escort her back home!

She was happy knowing her sister was out of the woods after their mother's passing. All her old anxieties on the torment she withheld, had abated. Dr Keefe Daly's move to Australia was what Grace needed, a like-minded soul. Both were passionate about medical science and die-hard workaholics in their research and care of their patients.

Patience asked Ming to wake her in an hour. She intended being alert for the arrival.

The captain was a woman with an English accent, she announced that there was turbulence ahead, passengers were to sit tight, and instructed not to release their seat belts until advised to do so. She wished them a pleasant flight and added in a jovial tone.

'Eat, drink and be merry, ladies!'

Patience nudged Ming.

'I told you this feels like ladies' night.'

2

———

TURBULENCE

The luxurious flight to Thailand had ample leg room, a lounge, bar, and coffee area. This had Ming and Patience speculating on what to expect at their destination.

'My goodness, it sure feels like we've died and gone to heaven already. Can you imagine what the resort in Thailand is going to be like?'

Patience, known for her exuberance, enjoyed surprises and could not contain her delight.

Ming looked at her with a quiet smile.

'Well, while I might agree with you, I am still a little cautious, especially when things look too good to be true, knowing I haven't paid much to have it that good. Don't mean to burst your bubble, just tread carefully.'

Patience listened to Ming's sage advice which felt like having Grace beside her. Poor Grace, she always looked for the potholes in every situation.

'I'm glad I have your common sense to count on, Ming.'

'To quote, my dear uncle Chen, in Cape Town, his business mind is always cautioning, 'less is more,' so let's see. This is a short flight, about two and a half hours, three hours in total, I think. Let's enjoy this before the workshops begin.'

'It could be longer, the captain said there's turbulence ahead, so that has to be factored into the time of arrival.'

'True. It's the first time I'm flying with a female captain. This is going to be quite a different experience.'

'Yes, for me too. Tell me a bit about your teaching life.'

'I teach in a rural community, it's a school for girls that I set up five years ago. I was born and raised in a rural community and wanted to give back to those who cannot attend the International Schools in my country. I struggled with funding, but some organisations have now come on board.'

'You are doing humanitarian work, what a wonderful way to give back! I have the utmost respect for teachers, they are the blood of society, educating, inspiring and guiding the future. A student never forgets the teachers who see the light within them. I'm so glad we've met, I foresee many enlightening conversations in our days together.'

'The work you're doing is humanitarian too. It would be interesting to know what the other women around us are doing in their lives. No doubt, the line of work we're in is the reason why we've been selected for this mission.' Ming frowned, still apprehensive about the months she had committed to.

AN HOUR LATER, the cabin lights flickered. The captain announced that they were approaching turbulent conditions and might hit the eye of a storm ahead.

'Ladies, remain in your seats please, this ride might be rough, keep those seat belts fastened.'

A clanging sound was emitted from inside the aircraft as it swayed and dipped, a few overhead lockers spewed out its contents, missing some passengers, and landing on others.

There was another urgent announcement from the captain.

'Ladies, this flight will be diverted to avoid any further destructive turbulence, your safety is our priority. Stay where you are until further advice.'

Patience looked at Ming whose eyes were shut tight, her head bowed, and her lips moving in a silent prayer. She glanced around, an Indian national rolled her rosary through her fingers with anxious speed. She swayed and chanted in a whispered voice. An older, Italian woman continued to make the sign of the cross, in rapid, repetitive motion, muttering *Caro Dio*. Others were a picture of stunned fear. The clanging sound subsided, but the swaying continued. A young stewardess walked out into the aisle, clutching onto the seats to stay on her feet with the erratic dipping motion. She handed out warm face-cloths and repeated softly to each passenger:

'Keep calm, we are going to be fine, relax. Take a few deep breaths.'

Behind her stepped an older stewardess with a broad smile and a tray of mini chocolates that she tossed around the cabin. Patience knew that this was to distract the passengers, to avoid an escalation in stress levels.

Soon the dizzy swaying stopped. The captain's posh English accent wafted over the airwaves.

'We appear to have moved away from the storm, but cannot be sure that it will not recur. As a precautionary measure, please hand over all mobile phones, laptops and tablets, essentially, all electronic devices, including wrist watches. This is, as I said, a precautionary measure to avoid further aviation disturbance.'

The cabin crew who also co-piloted the flight, walked around with plastic bags labelled with passengers' names. Patience thought it odd that they were not trusted to turn off their devices.

She looked at a panicked Ming rummaging through her handbag for her mobile phone.

'Do you find this strange? This rule has never applied on any commercial flight I've taken, even when the turbulence was crazier than what we just experienced.'

'I suppose this is a 'special' flight, so different rules.'

'It's odd, the captain, and stewardesses seem nice enough, but something does not sit well with me. The shutters are down on all windows, and the instruction was not to lift them. Have you noticed that the internal lights are out in the passengers' section but not in the stewardess area? There's no in-flight movie or flight path access. Please, I don't mean to frighten you, it's just rather unusual to have only part of the aircraft plunged in darkness.'

Ming knew what Patience was saying made sense, but she was not going to allow herself to be gripped by fear.

'We are going to be just fine, wait and see. I know we are on this flight for a reason, a design and purpose which will come to light soon.'

'Yeah, I should not assume the worst, I've been excited about this mission.' Her subdued tone and quiet acceptance were out of character for the feisty, Patience Sharvin.

Once all devices were collected, the captain's voice breezed through again.

'Thank you ladies, for your understanding on this matter. You may unfasten your seat belts. Zuri and Xandria are bringing through glasses of champagne. We need to celebrate that we are alive and well!'

'I don't drink, alcohol,' Ming said, 'I told them so during the interview.'

'They won't remember that, we can tell them when they come over to us.'

Zuri, the young stewardess, handed Patience a glass. She looked over at Ming and addressed her by name.

'Ming, this is your non-alcoholic beverage.'

'That's amazing, I didn't think anybody would have taken note.' Ming squealed.

Zuri smiled and moved to the next passenger.

'Bloody unbelievable, right? You didn't place an order... I'm telling you we're in for more surprises on this trip!'

An uneasiness enveloped Patience after her delighted outburst. She had to agree that this felt too good, too soon.

'The flight seems longer than we anticipated. We should go to the passengers' lounge to chat with others. Are you keen to do that?'

'You go ahead Patience, I want to meditate for half an hour.'

'Certainly, I'll fill you in when I get back.'

Patience walked into the lounge at the back of the aircraft. There was a bar to the right, and a coffee counter to the left, boasting a display of pastries and mini gourmet sandwiches. A few women milled around the bar sipping champagne, chatting. Others sat on luxurious, yellow leather couches, in earnest conversation. The cocktail party scene was another surprise. Patience looked at the pastries from across the lounge. She ignored the temptation to savour one and grabbed the vacant spot on the couch. She had to get in on the conversation. It was about time she found out what she had let herself in for.

Everybody turned to her as she introduced herself.

'Patience Sharvin, social worker from Australia.'

After a round of introductions, she realised the conversation was on the unexpected extended flying hours.

The Indian delegate, Akanya Das, a web developer with a broad smile, and a black dot dead centre on her forehead, looked at Patience wanting to strike up a conversation.

'My goodness, I almost wet my pants when the plane was swaying. I thought that's it, we're done for, forget seeing loved ones again. I was really, really scared, you know.' She patted her chest with each 'really' she uttered.

'Quite honestly, we are all in the same boat, it's not knowing what lies below, when airborne, that petrifies us.' Patience offered this consolation to the stressed Akanya.

The other women nodded in agreement and laughed, now that the moment had passed.

'We will certainly have a lot to tell our families when we get back home. My colleagues are intrigued by this mission. They think I'm very brave, indeed!' Akanya laughed.

A level of ease started to settle among them. Patience sensed Akanya's desire to feel part of the pack.

'My sister thinks I'm a crazy bird to have accepted being on this mission. No doubt we will have a lot to say after three months.' Patience added to support Akanya's obvious agitation.

She was happy everybody presented their expectations and concerns. Her final assumption was that everyone was happy they had signed up, and eager to get started with the training.

Patience went back to her seat to find Ming asleep. She mused on the benefits of meditation, taking note to tell Grace she saw the therapeutic value of meditation in inducing sleep.

Although Grace had greater peace of mind now, after several sessions with her therapist, sleep could be problematic for her when least expected. She loved herbal tea, Rooibos, being her favourite, but Chamomile was more frequently taken on those sleepless nights.

Patience picked up her book and continued reading.

3

———

THE ARRIVAL

What had started out as the expectation of a brief flight from Singapore to Thailand took many more hours. Passengers on board this luxurious machine had no idea what the time was, nor how many hours had passed.

Ming woke up confused. The penny dropped when she saw Patience in the seat next to her. She was mid-air somewhere. She felt the urgency to let her colleagues know her arrival at the expected destination was delayed.

'Good morning, Ming!' Patience chirped, 'I'm assuming it's morning, you slept like a baby. You must be starved, you missed the last meal. I dare not say, last night, as I have not the foggiest idea where we are, or the time of day.'

A crackling sound and the captain's relaxed, cheerful voice greeted the passengers.

'Hello again ladies, we have an hour to our destination. A treat awaits you after this diversion in our flight arrangements. I hope you had a relaxing few hours. I will begin the descent shortly. Stretch your legs, while you can. Tea and coffee will be served with some nibbles to tide you over until the banquet which is scheduled a few hours after we land.'

'Banquet?' Patience shot a quizzical look at Ming. I want to know where we are. The captain must be part of this program.'

'Yes, I'm not sure if I'm ready for a banquet. Hopefully, we will be informed about where we are and meet the captain in person soon. It seems a little mysterious and unsettling.'

'I think, we're so conditioned to having control of what we do, and where we do it, that these changes are making us uncomfortable. Might be part of the resilience training we were informed about in the interview session. Although I say 'informed,' it was rather sketchy.'

'After working in such a structured environment, this is different. Resilience training is good. I could take this back to my students. They need to learn to relax and enjoy their learning. I'm trying to break the cycle of repetitive, memory recall in favour of critical thinking. Girls struggle with this, in my rural community.'

'I don't deny that the experience will be beneficial, I abhor the secrecy, that's all. I don't doubt the value you can take back to your school. I need to calm my inner cynic.'

Patience had to be in the know if she was to perform at her optimum. She was paralysed when she faced the unknown. Both her mothers teased her about her 'tell me now' insistence as a child.

The captain called for everyone to be strapped in, the descent was about to begin. A woman in the next row from Patience had awful ear pressure, her fingers were tightly locked into her ear holes. She chewed like a millstone, eager to thwart the piercing pain shooting through her ears.

The descent was quite sharp, the aircraft appeared to be tilted as it dropped. To the left, the Italian with the rosary appeared to be in full incantation, her lips moved with vigour in her audible chant. Patience thanked her lucky stars that there were no wailing babies that needed to be pacified.

The expected rough landing was a surprisingly soft, almost cushioned one.

The captain announced that they would be called out alphabetically and Xandria would lead them into the building. A buzz of disgruntled tired voices rolled through the cabin.

An American called out,

'That will take longer to disembark. Why can't we leave as we are seated?'

The captain answered that there was an efficient reason for this process.

Patience whispered across to Ming.

'Hey, Ming Xu, this must feel like a school roll call to you. You are going to be here for a while.' Ming stood upright, staring ahead, afraid to speak.

'I'll wait for you Ming, it's going to be okay. See you soon.'

Patience left the cabin when surnames beginning with 'S' were called out, 'Sayed, Scott, Seymour, Sharvin...'

A subdued, steady, shuffling of women moved to the exit, with heads bowed until Patience erupted.

'Xandria! Are we going to get our mobile phones back as we get off the aircraft?'

A hushed whisper flittered around until the American voice was heard again.

'Yeah, Xandria, we need to call our people, this flight took longer than they would have expected. We need to assure them we are safe.'

'When we get in, not long now.' Xandria assured.

Patience heard the American woman say in a whisper, intended to be loud enough to be heard.

'Now, that was a true politician's response!'

A murmured giggle rippled through.

Patience giggled with the others, thinking this might end up being a fun-filled trip, after all, with the colourful personalities on board. Whatever this was going to be, she knew she would return to her role at her, Sisters Helping Sisters Organisation (SHSO), with greater skills. This had to be the positive outcome she yearned. For a fleeting second she considered whether Grace was concerned about her lack of communication, at all, with the suave Keefe Daly in the picture. Her sister was her soul sister, they were joined at the hip. Nothing would separate them, not even the dashing, Dr Keefe Daly, newly out of Ireland.

With no inkling whether it was night or day, the women entered the enclosed walkway. They assumed they were walking into the airport arrivals area. At the end of the walkway, a steep metal stairway, somewhat like a fire exit, greeted them. The first woman stopped — a voice urged her from below, to step down. They scuttled like mice, afraid and eager.

They entered what appeared to be a large reception area to an entertainment centre or the foyer to a gigantic hotel.

Ming made her way towards Patience, her stunned face oozed with distress. They were handed warm face-cloths and a cocktail.

'I told you this might feel like I died and went to heaven, don't look so serious. Relax! This is more pampering than I've ever had in such quick succession, in my adult life.'

'I wish I could, I feel odd. My chakras are out of whack. I need an empty space to meditate. I need my phone, my mantras are...' Ming stopped when she realised two women were staring at her.

'I'm sure that will be possible soon, I doubt we are in an airport, it feels different, but I can't explain why it's different.'

Zuri stood on a platform with a microphone, ready to make an announcement.

'Good evening ladies, welcome to your three months in God's country where you will gain the finest guidance in your chosen fields and leave blessed to uplift the lot of women to greater heights. You will be escorted to your quarters. A banquet is scheduled at 7.30 pm. You will be notified where to go. For now, breathe, relax and enjoy. Collect your labelled bag off the table at the end of the room. That is the attire you will wear tonight for the banquet. A name badge is included in the pack, please ensure you are wearing it at all times. I will lead you out, your room doors are labelled with your names. There are no keys to any of the doors — you are in a safe environment. God's country.'

The American woman was flustered.

'Where is this place, Zuri?'

Zuri bowed, smiled and responded.

'The captain will address everyone at the banquet, reserve your questions until then. For now, Alexis, Xandria and I will lead you to the residential quarters.'

'Mmmm... well, this gets stranger by the minute... we could be on Mars, for all we know!' the American hissed.

Akanya piped in, 'I think we should reserve our comments for the captain, that's the sensible thing to do.'

'It's like being back in school. We get uniforms and name badges. You will feel right at home here, Ming.' Patience joked, in her usual way, as she did with Grace.

Ming was stoic, unresponsive, her quiet manner placed her in a bubble that shut everything out.

As Patience expected their rooms were alphabetically delineated, Ming Xu was down on the other end of the corridor from her.

THE ROOMS WERE COMPACT. A single, narrow bed, tiny shower within a space-age dome structure and a boxed-in toilet, made for an elf. A small microwave and kettle sat on a tray table. Patience observed that there was no television, just a little desk with a telephone. She rushed to the desk to call Grace. She stopped - she had no idea, like the other hundred and forty-nine women, where she was or what the time difference would be, to call Australia. Grace could be sound asleep, or at work.

She wanted to linger in the shower for the cascading hot water to soothe her aching body, but struggled to move around in the tight space. Her shower at home was large enough for a whole family at once!

She got out to dress when she heard the announcement.

'Ladies, you have half an hour to get to the banquet, the walk to the banquet hall will take ten minutes from your quarters, please be punctual.'

Patience contemplated what role the captain had in this set-up. The voice on the intercom was that of the captain. Her unmistakable English accent was a dead giveaway. Serene ducted music created a calm atmosphere. Patience unpacked the bag she was handed. In it was a large flowing white kaftan and her name badge. Just her first name and the distinct gold-plated letters **T U C**, to the left of her name.

She felt a rising dread, sensing she might be caught in the web of a cult mission. What on earth was **T U C**?

She stepped outside her room when a buzzer was sounded. Quiet rows of women, all dressed in white flowing kaftans, floated along the corridor, their badges sparkling in the dim light.

Patience muttered under breath.

'Weirder by the minute, brides of Frankenstein! Heaven help us all!'

4
____

THE BANQUET

A distant sound of jingling bells cascaded through the banquet hall creating a Christmasy feeling. The faint fragrance of lavender incense lingered in the air. Large, Bohemian, crystal chandeliers hung low from the ceiling, giving the room an elegant, exotic charm. Despite the hedonistic appeal of the room, everything looked new, fresh, unused and designed to seduce.

Kaftans billowed in a gentle caress around the women as they walked in. They were eager yet nervous and unsure of what to expect, a spiritual aura permeated the room.

Patience was silent until they were seated. She turned to Ming.

'Died and went to heaven, I said, right?'

'Certainly appears that way,' Ming whispered, 'except it feels like a grand funeral.'

Akanya looked at them, the admonishment obvious in her eyes.

'Ladies let us be gracious guests this evening. We need to know what we have let ourselves in for,' she whispered across the table, leaning forward, ensuring she was heard.

'Yes, you're right Akanya, I will have to keep a check on my comments, but I'm warning you, it won't be easy,' Patience added with her usual honesty.

A circular platform and a lone microphone was at the front of the room.

Everybody was silent.

A TALL, oval-faced woman, with long, black hair floating against her yellow kaftan walked with a brisk stride and stepped onto the circular platform. She bowed, smiled and surveyed the room.

'Good evening, chosen ones, how lovely to see you all, so beautiful and serene. I am Masuyo, welcome to your home for the next three months.' Her British accent finally had a face.

Patience nudged Ming.

'The captain, who would have thought!'

Ming stared at the captain in disbelief.

Akanya looked across at Patience, the message was clear that she should shut up.

'I see the surprise in some of your faces. Yes I am the captain that flew you in, and I will head the operations on the ground. Xandria, Alexis and Zuri will be your guides throughout the process.

The American raised her hand.

'Where exactly are we? It was a long flight, much longer than is usual so when can we have our cell phones back?'

'Save your questions for the Q & A after dinner, please,' Masuyo said with a bow. She looked up with raised, arched eyebrows, making everyone aware of the authority she wielded.

All movement quietened.

Patience knew it was just a matter of time before Akanya clashed with the American, if she chose to assume a mothering, chastising attitude towards her.

'Firstly, before we go any further, I will explain what T U C means, the inscription on your name badge.' Masuyo smiled with a calm benevolent aura visible in her changeable manner, voice, and facial expression. She exuded a deep humility in this moment.

Patience pondered whether this was an act on the first night, but could not fathom how such a woman would have a mercurial nature. There was undoubtedly a spiritual air about her that commanded the same response.

'T U C represents the core of our purpose in Truth, Understanding and Compassion, our T U C values as women today and into the future.'

A soft, 'aaah' sigh and nodding of heads made Masuyo smile like the sun at high noon. Her face glowed at the positive response to T U C as fundamental to the organisation.

'This is how we shall treat all who we encounter, every day, in every waking, breathing moment of our existence. With T U C, there will be no war, no hatred, no judgement, just peace. You have been living T U C values without quite knowing it, that is the reason why you are here today, the chosen ones to fulfil a higher purpose. I will leave that there for now and continue after dinner. Zuri, Xandria, and Alexis will now serve dinner.'

A tantalising aroma of seafood, roasted potatoes, and extra-cheesy lasagna wafted into the banquet room as Masuyo's three assistants walked around, serving a hungry mob of women. The jingling bells stopped, a light instrumental combination of sounds with the distinct soft melody of a piano could be heard. The mood was set for an enjoyable evening. With a glass of wine down, the ladies were relaxed, the conversation and laughter flowed.

'This is not so bad after all, right?' Akanya smiled, her head bobbing with delight. 'Everything is provided and we will be trained further to return even better at the jobs we are doing at home. Three months will fly, you'll see.' Her circular, lotus flower grand hand gesture when she said, 'even better,' was lost, nobody within earshot responded.

After dinner, coffee was served in the large boardroom, adjacent to the dining hall.

A pleasant social atmosphere surrounded them. The American woman walked up to Patience and Ming.

'Hello ladies, I've been wanting to get acquainted with you both, but things are moving pretty quickly around here, after that delayed flight.'

Patience looked at the woman's name badge, she valued addressing people by name to ensure the person she was talking to, knew that they mattered.

'Nice to meet you, Audra, I'm Patience and this is Ming.'

'Great to meet you both, so what do you think about what we've let ourselves in for. I have a few questions to shoot during the Q & A session later. How about you?'

'I'm giving this a chance, I signed up for the offer it presented. I have a question or two on a few matters,' Patience said.

'What about you?' Audra looked at Ming.

Patience made sure she reiterated that names were important.

'Ming, I think Audra is looking for an ally.'

'No, no, not an ally, just trying to figure out the thinking among the ladies.'

'I'm here for a purpose and want the skills the organisation is offering, so I will give it my best shot.' Ming spoke with a soft voice, forcing Audra to move closer to hear her.

'Interesting that no men are on this mission, although I bet a man might be behind this operation.' Audra laughed.

'I won't bet on that, Audra, I think we are in for a few more pleasant surprises. Look at this place, it's almost a city or like being on board a luxury cruise liner! Well, except for that darn pokey shower.'

'Yeah, I agree the shower is not the best, but the place is amazing. I wish I knew where I was.' Audra added.

Ming remained in meditative silence, barely listening to Audra's chatter.

They stood around, greeting and introducing themselves until Zuri announced that everyone should take their seats, the Q & A was about to begin.

'WELCOME BACK LADIES,' Masuyo smiled, looking around the room.

'You will have a full tour of the place in the morning. There's a gym, library, coffee shop, mini supermarket, indoor park, and Olympic size swimming pool. Each day of the week offers something different by way of training, a timetable will be left outside your room on your breakfast tray. Please ensure you make your selection of what you want to train in each day and pop it in the mailbox in the foyer. There are some compulsory modules to cover, but more of that in the days ahead. Let's begin with each of you standing up and saying your name, for a sense of familiarity among us. In the forthcoming days, you will no doubt get to know each other on a more personal, intimate level. Understanding is key. Let's begin at the back of the room.'

A scraping sound of chairs and muffled voices filled the room.

'I appeal to you to listen with care to each name, it ithe respect we accord each other as part of our T U C values.'

Beautiful English names, cultural names, exotic names were heard. Patience looked at each person, ranging from around twenty to perhaps sixty, she surmised.

'Thank you all, what a wonderful array of names, we shall look at the meanings behind your names in one of our sessions. Alexis, Zuri and Xandria will walk around with microphones to have your questions aired. Let's begin with a show of hands. Audra's hand was the first one up, followed by Akanya. Numbers were allocated for the order in which questions would be addressed.

Ming bent over to look at Patience.

'You're right, it's just like being in school.'

Audra asked, 'where are we and when can we have our cell phones back?'

'You will not be told where we are stationed for our safety and security. For now, accept that you are safe and well taken care of. Phones will not be returned yet, so you have to be patient on that request.' Masuyo explained, her voice low and deliberate.

'But, we need to contact our families,' Audra insisted.

'Please hold back your comments until we've addressed the order in which the questions have come up. You've had your first question addressed.'

Akanya was next in line.

'Firstly I would like to thank one and all for this opportunity. I already feel I am on holiday in this beautiful place. I agree we should be patient,' she glanced at Audra and continued. 'I want to know, what exactly, is our 'empowerment' to be, as per the interview?' Her head bobbed a lot faster conveying her nervousness.

'Good question. You all have committed to uplifting women in your respective societies, that is why you were chosen as hand-picked individuals, to take our mission forward in line with your current work.'

Patience was third and used the opportunity to extend on Masuyo's response.

'What happens after the three months, do we go back to our lives and sever the links with the mission? A lot has been vested in us so I feel there is more to this?'

'Discerning question. After the three months, you will be placed in a community for three to six months, or longer, that is if you commit to training young women in disadvantaged locations. This is to develop a level of confidence in them as possible future leaders of their communities and globally.'

Many women stood up, agitated that they were not aware that their tenure went beyond the three months.

'Settle down please, I will explain.' Masuyo announced.

She commanded the room in her ability to offer reasons with the skill of a mother calming her fretful baby — quiet, soft, gentle, free of agitation.

'You have the option to leave after three months or commit to paying back in three to six months service at a designated location where all your personal needs will be met. You cannot opt out now because your three month contractual agreement is in operation.'

One anxious voice shouted from the left side of the room,

'So you intend to hold us hostage here for three months!'

Unfazed by the outburst, Masuyo looked in the direction of the last comment.

'Not a hostage at all, look around you, how can that be true? You are free to leave after three months. That is the only binding clause that you all signed up for.'

A fourth speaker asked.

'Where are these locations that we might be placed in, should we choose to stay on in service, that is?'

'A relevant question, those locations will be highlighted in the days ahead, and you have the option to decline our choice of placement. We are happy to work with what makes you comfortable.'

Mumbles emerged from each part of the room.

Masuyo declared the session over saying she was happy to address more questions at a later stage.

'Have a relaxing night ladies, breakfast will be served in your rooms tomorrow to allow you a bit of a sleep-in. Please fill in the breakfast card before you retire tonight. Thank you for being here, anything new is stressful, but remember you will be igniting the flame of Truth, Understanding and Compassion. Good night ladies.'

A quiet parade of ladies strolled back to their rooms.

Patience was happy to commit to what she had signed up for.

She knew many questions would be answered as the days unfolded.

Grace was her concern, she would be sick with worry, by this stage, not having heard from her.

5

COMMITMENT

Patience was wide awake for several hours after the banquet, pondering on the reactions of the women. She had a gnawing feeling that resistance from some quarters of the chosen women would incite tension. Power is a prized possession — when perceived as taken away, it unleashes an unpleasant side in people. She mulled over power agendas and its erosion of relationships. Husbands and wives at her SHSO, bosses, and managers, teachers, politicians, criminals, parents, children — every facet of life.

Audra appeared to be brash in how she handled change, Akanya assumed, as an older woman, she could issue unsolicited advice to others. Yet deep down, Patience knew Audra and Akanya would not be the ladies who would start a revolt against the mission. She fell asleep, thinking about Grace and Keefe, wondering if they had struck up a romantic bond. Grace was reluctant to commit to acknowledging this.

THE SOUNDS OF A TRICKLING WATERFALL, chirping birds and the

smell of freshly percolated coffee, tickled Patience's senses, making her stretch and roll around the luxurious covers in contentment. She put out her breakfast order later than the others last night. French toast, baked beans, a few slices of avocado and haloumi greeted her at the door. A heated tray and a thin tubular vase with one white tulip and a card attached read, 'Good morning, have a happy day,' with the gold-lettered T U C beneath it. She was amazed that the mission might have known what her favourite flower was, or was it pure coincidence? Next to the tray was a pack of clothes, labelled, 'daywear.'

She tucked into her breakfast, and reached for her phone in her handbag, pulling back when she remembered it was taken. Well, Grace will have to wait until I'm told I can call her, she thought, hoping Grace knew she was safe. She said it out aloud, 'I am safe girl. My thoughts are that you should not worry about me.' She hoped this mental conversation would register with Grace just as it used to when they were children.

She showered, turning in little quarter pirouettes as she manoeuvred her way in the compact space. She pulled out the blue tracksuit and sneakers, the tracksuit was soft, breathable and comfortable. It moulded around her like a second skin. Patience was grateful for the leisurely morning, it gave her the space to gather her thoughts and rest after the hectic journey to this unknown destination. They were due to meet in the conference room at ten o' clock for a tour of this vast oasis. She secretly nicknamed it, 'The Mother Ship.'

A tinkle of wind chimes indicated that it was time to head off to the conference room. An index card mapped the direction to the venue. Patience thought about the tranquil setting, the beautiful morning sounds, the tinkling wind chimes, and wondered if these were included because Masuyo was Japanese and whether she was the sole commander of the mission.

Women strolled along in pale-blue and pale-green tracksuits, greeting each other with an air of respect. Ming hurried towards Patience.

'Did you rest well, Patience?'

'I did eventually, it took a long time to doze off, how about you?'

'I slept very well after meditating. I feel far more relaxed this morning.'

'Great to hear that Ming, yes that's the way we need to approach our time here.'

Zuri, Alexis and Xandria greeted them at the door. Masuyo was nowhere to be seen. Their names were ticked off, they were handed a bottle of water and a little bag of nuts and raisins. Patience asked Ming if she received a white tulip with her breakfast.

'No, I got a beautiful orchid, my favourite flower, I transplant them at home and have a vast collection that I love handing out on special occasions.'

'Interesting, very interesting indeed. I received my favourite too. I will ask one of the others what they received. I don't remember being asked about my preference in flowers, do you?'

'No, that question was not asked. Seems strange. How would they know?

'It's a thoughtful gesture, I suppose we should not look a gift horse in the mouth.'

'I love that English expression, 'look a gift horse in the mouth,' it's so complicated I think, the word 'ungrateful' is more effective. I can't associate gifts and horses in my brain, although I think horses are majestic creatures.' Ming mused.

Patience laughed until tears rolled down her cheeks, 'I've not laughed this much since I last saw my sister! Thank god for you Ming, you will keep me happy, for sure.'

'I'm glad you found that amusing, but you have to admit, the English language is very confusing for one whose mother-tongue is not English.'

'Hey Ming, you speak the Queen's English, your grammar is perfect, no doubt about that!'

'We are very strict about speaking English the correct way if we choose to speak it.'

They seemed to be the only two who were comfortable and happy that morning. Zuri addressed them.

'Good morning everyone, you all look fresh and happy, and might I add, so lovely in your blue and green outfits. There's a reason for the choice of colours, those in blue will follow me on the tour of the centre and those in green will follow Xandria. We have two hours for this tour, then a light lunch and another address from Masuyo after lunch. You will have private time from 2 pm until dinner is served at 6 pm. Use this time to socialise with each other and please use the facilities available in your new, although, temporary home.'

MING AND PATIENCE were split up on the tour, Ming went off with Xandria and her group, Patience joined Zuri. Audra sidled up to Patience for a chat.

'How are you? Patience? Hope I got your name right?'

'Yes, Audra, I'm Patience, I'm good this morning, and how are you?'

'I'm good too, just need to talk to my people soon, you know.'

'Yeah, that is the tough bit about being here, I suppose.'

'Are you going to accept it or are you going to ask a few questions?'

'I will ask when the time is right, I don't want to ruffle any feathers? But, if I feel I'm imprisoned by 'Big Brother,' or in our case, 'Big Sister,' I will shake things up. For now, there is no reason to be disgruntled. Remember the slogan, T U C, I love the thinking behind that.'

'That's strategic Patience, your name says it all, and you have a good sense of humour. I might adopt the same attitude, you're sensible.'

'I am my mothers' daughter. That has carried me through some pretty tough times.'

'I would love to get to know more about you.'

'Likewise Audra. We should listen in to Zuri, now.'

THE TOUR WAS SPECTACULAR, a mini supermarket for anything one desired from confectionery, baked goods, toiletries, soft drinks, and magazines, a few other grocery needs and a range of fresh fruit. A well-stocked bar and a coffee shop with every type of coffee for the discerning coffee lover. A library, a park area, a gym, spa, two large swimming pools, a massage parlour, two movie theatres, one showing contemporary films, and the other twentieth century and pre-twentieth century films. A hair-dressing and beauty salon with fortnightly appointments, grabbed Patience's attention, knowing that she could not expect hair braiding and beading or her coiffed up-styles at this salon. Everything was available to mimic a pampered lifestyle. Television screens were fitted in all conference rooms with no desktop computers in sight. Her thoughts slipped back to the time she was held at the Zulu chief's compound in South Africa, all those years ago. This was five star treatment, and she was not abducted, she chose to accept the offer presented to her.

After the two hour tour, they headed back to the conference room to meet Masuyo.

'GOOD DAY LADIES, it's good to see you are becoming acquainted with your new surroundings. Should you require anything more, please ask Alexis, Xandria, or Zuri to put in your request. We are grateful that you accepted our offer to make a difference now and into the next generation, on how this world is governed. Too much has been mishandled, T U C has been absent, hence the violation against humanity. You are in Stage One of garnering skills. Some skills that you are already well versed in, to empower young women to rise as leaders tomorrow, to govern the lands of their birth or seek out other countries, to end the torment they have long endured.' Masuyo spoke with quiet dignity and passion.

The women rose in respect of her vision, applauding her passion for change.

Patience believed the conversion of the stubborn and resistant was already in process. Perhaps there won't be any rebels after all. Feminist passion burst forth with a commitment to the cause. She said a silent prayer of gratitude for what appeared to be a clear path ahead.

Masuyo was pleased that the tails of resistance appeared to be down.

'While you might not have your mobile devices, you may write a letter a week which will be mailed for you to your loved ones. There is a self-service post shop to the left of this area where writing paper, postage stamps and envelopes are available. It might sound antiquated to some of you who have not written a letter in a very long time.'

Audra smiled and nudged Patience.

'That's good eh!'

'It sure is. I'm happy with that, at least my sister will know I'm alive.'

Alexis, Zuri and Xandria wheeled in large tables decked with an assortment of sandwiches, tea, coffee, soft drinks, and pastries.

'Once we are over with your light lunch, you are free to wander around the complex at leisure until dinner time. If you are lost at any time, proceed to the end of the corridor where you will find a red telephone. Press zero and follow the prompts to get back to your room, or any other part of the complex.'

Some went back to their rooms, others went to the library. Patience asked Audra and Ming to join her in the bar for a glass of wine.

'I don't have any alcohol, remember,' Ming said, 'you go ahead with Audra.'

'There are fresh juices in the bar too, come along, I'm not letting you get away this time,' Patience coerced.

'A glass of citrus juice is what I need, so thank you, I will join you.'

'I hope we get to know a few more ladies this afternoon. There are a hundred and twenty countries, I think, represented here. Not too sure about that though, but that's a lot of 'getting to know you' to do.'

The air was socially casual that afternoon. Everyone strolled around, introducing themselves, squealing with delight when they found they shared passions, ideals, and visions, or knew the same people in the outside world. Familiarity brought congeniality, the need to feel accepted was primal.

Hope returned on day two of a three month mission.

6

OUTSIDE

Four days had passed since Grace heard from Patience. Her mind flitted back to almost twenty years ago when Patience was abducted by the Zulu chief's henchmen as one of his prized concubines. She contained her anxiety, not wanting Keefe to be put off by her overreactions to the situation.

Her relationship with Keefe filled a gnawing void in her life, a void that had grown so wide with each year, since her mother's untimely death. Now, she was not as lonely and isolated as she was, but, her life as a doctor still took precedence in her world. They shared their medical vision and made time to grow close, tapping into each other's personal worlds in striving to achieve balance in their workaholic lives.

She started the relationship with Dr Keefe Daly with tentative uncertainty. Being out of the relationship game since her last high school fling, made her wary. The dapper Dr Andrew Lang, her young intern, now assistant head of ER, vied for her attention, and much hoped for, reciprocal affection — she kept the fortress to her heart locked then. They maintained a good friendship, he made her feel young and carefree. She saw him at work, two nights a week. Their ER shifts were split since his promotion.

She put in a strong motivation for his promotion and was relieved when he was appointed to be her assistant.

Keefe's quiet nature, his emotionality and profound adoration for his mother, appealed to Grace. It gave her the space to continue with her own passions. He never complained about being ill nor tired and accepted the social activities she planned for them, without a fuss.

This was a whole new ball game for her, she was reclusive for many years, concealing her fear and shame from curious eyes — now with Keefe by her side, she filled most of their days off with going to the theatre, taking drives to the Blue Mountains or spending the odd two days at Mollymook, a picturesque beach haven in the Ulladulla region of New South Wales. She loved it, the no crowds, peaceful, slow, laid-back place. The days spent there made her feel safe enough to take lone walks on the beach — something she had not done in over two decades. Past fears lurked in the shadowy hinterland of memory.

With each day spent together, she felt the shared closeness develop between them. She adored his accent, the way he caressingly said her name, and that he was considerate and giving.

Felicity Cassano, Patience's close friend and business associate, warned her against men like Keefe, saying they were married to their professions, grog, and football. How wrong she was about Keefe! Felicity gave Grace the worst scenario on any of her choices in life. She kept happy and silent that all Felicity had told her to expect in her relationship with Keefe, was non-existent. Keefe, although reserved in nature, loved his long chats with Grace, this filled the gap she felt when Patience left for her six-month sojourn. She knew her mother would have approved of Keefe as a good partner for her. They were well-suited in their vision of life and their commitment to saving lives.

Busy nights at the Emergency Room preoccupied her, keeping her from tipping over the edge in her anxiety for Patience's safety. Keefe was a level-headed man who had the ability to keep her calm and grounded. She had to tell him about her fears relating to Patience's past problems. She toyed with the idea, not wanting to expose Patience's life, without her permission. The intimacy that had grown between them led to the decision that Keefe would move in with her, only once Patience returned. He was coming over for dinner that night, she knew she had to tell him about her concern for Patience.

'How was your day Grace?' He hugged her at the door, strolling to the lounge with his arm around her.

'I had a quiet day today, I've been trying to find information on this mission my sister has embarked on.'

'Still no word from her?' As a man of few words, he spoke only when it was necessary, with clear sensible intention. Grace appreciated his good sense. She enjoyed her quiet space, his personality meant she didn't have to significantly readjust her lifestyle.

'Yeah, nothing yet, so unlike her.'

'She might be settling in to her new routine, I'm sure she will call you soon.'

'I hope so. I'm in the dark about this mission, she was elusive about it, not quite knowing much about it herself. I've never wanted to smother her, but I'm afraid, I might have come across that way, with my exuberance in wanting to protect her.'

'Aye, all older sisters are guilty of this, my sister, Aileen, followed me throughout my life as a child, teenager, and young man. Her motherly concern was adorable, but, she had to pull back later if we were to continue having a good sibling relationship.'

'I understand what you're saying, but Patience and I share a relationship that defies the norm. I don't mean to be dismissive of what you're saying. I know wherever my sister is right now, she will be sick with worry in her concern for me. Just one call or text message is all I need, to know she arrived safely and is busy getting on with the deviation she made in her life.'

'Give it a full week Grace, then we can both delve into her whereabouts if you still haven't had news from her.'

Grace agreed, although her mind screamed, what if it's too late, so much could happen. She smiled at Keefe thanking him for his support. The last thing she wanted was to sound like a highly-strung middle-aged woman!

After a leisurely dinner, they settled down for a cuddle on the couch on this wet, chilly, Sydney evening. Half an hour later, her mobile phone buzzed. Keefe 's look questioned whether she was going to take the call in their intimate moment.

'It might be Patience, you know, I should check the message.'

It was a message from Andrew Lang, telling her to watch an ABC live press conference.

'Why would he want me to watch a press conference, it must be some medical matter, knowing him.'

'Turn it on Grace, I know you're curious.' Keefe laughed.

Singapore airport rolled into view in the background. Grace leaned forward, trying not to miss a word, clutching onto Keefe's arm.

The press conference was in full swing.

TONIGHT WE HAVE *confirmation that a flight set to arrive in Thailand four days ago, has not been seen since its departure. Contact with the tower was lost an hour after take-off. Anxious families have contacted the airline for information on the whereabouts of their family. Nothing has come to light yet. It is alleged that all passengers on board are female. Information that has just come through indicates that the destination was Thailand for a three month training program — the nature of that program is not yet known. There will be hourly updates on this disturbing situation.*

KEEFE PULLED GRACE CLOSER. He put his hand on her head.

'Grace, this is just information at this stage, we are not going to jump the gun here, I think you should contact the number on the screen and give them Patience's details. We have to hang tight until we have more information.'

Grace felt her heart heave into her throat, her pulse pounded in every pressure point. She sat still for five minutes as thoughts raced through her mind. She hung onto Keefe's hand as she made the call.

'Hello, good evening. I'm responding to the news briefing I saw on the ABC now. My sister, Patience Sharvin, a social worker, was on that flight to Thailand. I have not heard from her since her departure.' Grace gave the lady her contact details. No conversation to gather more information was possible. It was a hotline to report missing persons on board that fateful flight. Nobody cared about how she felt. She looked at Keefe, immobilised with fear.

'I'm so afraid Keefe... I don't think I can handle this... again.'

'It's early days, Grace, you must keep calm. You will have to remember everything Patience told you about this trip.'

'She was in a similar situation when she was abducted in South Africa. I will tell you about it, another day. The thing is, Patience did not say much about this program she signed up for. My fear is, when planes go missing, it's never a good outcome... I wish... I have tried calling her phone these past two days, it's switched off.'

'Who else would she have told about this venture?'

'Perhaps, Felicity and Virginia Bale, Virginia is running the Sisters Helping Sisters Organisation in her absence.

'First thing tomorrow morning, call Felicity and we can both go to see Virginia after you make that call. Another thing, I'm not leaving you alone tonight, Grace, I'm staying over. This couch is very comfortable.'

'Thank you,' Grace whispered. They both sat on the couch until sunrise. Keefe fell asleep while Grace lay awake, frozen with fear. How could she sleep when her sister was in danger? All she could think about was why did this happen, how much more was she going to be called to endure? She whispered with shut eyes, 'Please help me, mum, I need Patience, keep her safe, please...' Life had dealt them both cruel blows as young women - fear was always her first reaction while Patience fought on with optimism.

THE NEXT MORNING, Grace called Felicity in Melbourne. Felicity was close to Patience but critical of Grace — she expected Grace to be bold, brave and daring, not cautious and mellow as she presented.

'When did you say you last heard from Patience?'

'Four days ago.'

'You did not think to act on this earlier, you should have called me.'

'I had to give Patience her space to settle in what she's doing? I'm informing you now because there's confirmation she is missing.'

'Yes, yes, okay, I need more details to probe into this from my end. The more pressure we put on the authorities the better if we want rapid results.' Felicity's matter of fact attitude was no surprise.

'I think we should schedule a meeting with the media too, I might have to come to Sydney or you to Melbourne.'

'No, please hold off with the media involvement, we need more information.' Grace felt a cold chill pass through her, she detested invasion of her privacy.

'More information? Patience is missing, and we have no idea where she might be, whether she is fighting for her life or worse yet if she's dead.' Felicity bellowed down the phone. Grace heard Alf's soft voice in the background.

'Is something wrong love, has something happened?' Felicity

ignored his question. She told Grace she would be in touch, and plonked the phone down, leaving Grace as helpless as she was before the call.

'What did she say, Grace, I could hear her raised voice?'

'She's irate that I took this long to let her know, and she wants to get the media involved, here in Australia, I'm not keen to do this just yet.'

'Grace, one step at a time is necessary, but, the media might well dog you when all the dots connect to you. Brace yourself for that, please.'

Grace needed Keefe's calm wisdom after Felicity's blunt attack. She clung to the hope that she would be stronger in the days ahead with him close by her side.

LATER THAT DAY she went over with Keefe to see Virginia.

'What can I do to help, Dr Sharvin?'

'Please continue running things here for Patience as you have been doing, keep the sisters safe and happy, is all I ask.' She put her arm around Virginia as tears brimmed in her terrified eyes.

'And please call me, Grace, we are no longer doctor and patient. Let me know if you need additional help while we wait for more news before we act to expedite finding out what happened.'

Keefe kept in the background while Grace and Virginia tried to recall all Patience had said about the mission she had embarked on, only four days ago.

7

GRACE AND KEEFE

Six months after Grace and Keefe met in Amsterdam, at the medical conference in December of that year, and the strategic engineering of Nina Holstead's Cupid's arrow, they found a comfortable connection with each other — not the hormonal attraction of young love, but one founded on their mutual passion for healing, and the deep, quieter spirit of each other. And so Australia and Ireland merged forces for a well-served, skilled pair of medical practitioners.

Keefe bore no secrets, he was open about his past life. He was married briefly, a colossal error on his part, he admitted, thinking that a younger woman was what he needed after being a bachelor for many years, lost in his medical meanderings. He was not the partying type, inclined to be studious, preferring a quiet drink at home with a few mates or going to the theatre, and at times binging on a Netflix series. He enjoyed travelling, journeying to new cultural destinations every year. His extensive travel itinerary, spanning almost two decades, included remote islands and other forgotten gems around the world.

Grace confided in him regarding her challenges in South Africa with her harassment and final ordeal with Boetie Arendse.

She praised her therapist's ability to exorcise her mental torment, decades later. He listened in silence, shocked that there was no police involvement and that Grace chose to lock away her ordeal in fear and shame.

'You don't realise how strong you are. To have gone through what you have, and still lead a healthy, normal life, is an amazing feat. I recommend that you see the therapist at least twice a year, to air anything that niggles at you from the past. The mind is at times an unfathomable entity. We think we have it all under control, yet one setback, albeit unrelated to the specific memory, and the apparently quietened trauma comes gushing back. There's no shame in seeing a therapist in an ongoing arrangement as a medical practitioner yourself.' His tender genuine concern convinced her that she was fated to meet this man who filled her need as a friend, lover and the father-figure she lost in a horrendous attack during her early adulthood.

'I don't think of myself as strong at all, but it means a lot coming from you. Dr Deakin might be happy with the suggestion that I should see her at least twice a year. I remember being so anxious during my visits to her after my mum passed away. She put me at ease from the outset and I appreciated that she respected me as a medic first, and then her patient.'

'Aye, it's awkward when you're a medic and you need help. We are inclined to think we are beyond needing help or might be perceived as odd, or perhaps weak if we needed help!' This is because *we* think we are superhuman! His mellow laugh warmed her each time she heard it.

Their shared world grew more comfortable when he teased her about her South African-Aussie accent, and she teased his adorable Irish accent. The inner child surfaced in their tender moments.

From their first meeting at the medical conference in Amsterdam, all they had was two weeks to get to know each other, before Grace returned to Australia. He had already had an offer for a medical position prior to their first meeting. The magnetic tug he felt for Grace, confirmed his decision to take up the offer.

They spent hours on the telephone, getting to know each other more intimately, before he arrived in Australia. Grace was still self-conscious, in not wanting to have Skype chats or video calls with him. She confided in Patience about Keefe's suggestion to face-chat and her reservation about doing so. She thought back to Patience's pragmatic advice, although she too, lacked experience in matters of the heart.

She could almost hear Patience say, 'Grace, he needs to know you, warts and all, you should have some face-chats with him. Let him see you, *au naturel.*' Patience giggled and added, 'just not completely *au naturel,* please!'

She missed her sister with every ache of a sad heartbeat.

Keefe's week in Australia to sign the contract and prepare for his move from Belfast, strengthened the growing bond between them. He was to move into the doctors' lodgings at the hospital before he decided on a place of his own.

Three months later, he was planning a getaway with Grace, and close to moving in with her.

'I've been entertaining thoughts about taking a trip with you to Bali at the end of the year. What do you think?'

'Sounds marvellous. I do want to be home when Patience returns, is it possible to defer things until she gives me her return home details?'

Little did Grace know then, when Keefe was sounding out his Bali getaway that Andrew Lang would alert her to the press conference on Patience's missing flight.

Grace continued to attend her weekly yoga and self-enhance-ment classes which she had started after her final therapy session with Dr Deakin, over a year ago. She felt stronger mentally and emotionally. She took long hikes with Keefe on their weekends off — her emotions were in tatters now. It was difficult to put on a happy face when fear crept into her thoughts on her sister's whereabouts.

Deflated by the news that Patience had not landed in Thailand as scheduled had her struggling to find a way to avoid slipping back emotionally and psychologically — she had to summon the strength in the search for Patience. Her mother, Varuna, was no longer there to guide her. She battled with her demons, trying to avoid succumbing to thoughts that she and Patience were always going to be in a tussle for life's peace and harmony.

She had much to be grateful for, with Keefe's entrance into her life. She had given up on finding love at this stage of her life. Her mother's stoic life alone, without her father, after his tragic murder, made her want to go it alone, too. Her mother's gentle sobs late at night when she thought Grace and Patience were sound asleep, remained a living memory.

Hidden grief is a mask that shackles the soul, keeping the pain alive, embedded within, out of sight in its silent struggle.

Grace had word from the investigating authorities that an interview was scheduled in Canberra. A group of people wanted to start an action campaign with other countries. Andrew Lang offered to cover Grace's nights at ER during this time. Keefe took two days leave from work to accompany her to the meeting. She was unaware that more people from Australia had gone on the crusade Patience had chosen.

Two groups of people were already seated in the office when Keefe and Grace arrived.

One group hailed from North Queensland and the other from Tasmania.

The missing women, including Patience were in social services, one was a prison parole officer for women, and the other a counsellor and work placement officer at an orphanage. Everyone was in the dark as Grace was, on the actual nature of the campaign.

A female investigating officer posed the first question.

'Other than being solicited by email because of the work they were involved in, is there anything else you can tell us that might assist with finding and returning the missing passengers.'

Grace looked around, an eerie stillness made it quite clear that everyone had no specific details to share, or were silenced by the fear and dread they felt.

'My sister called me before she boarded the flight for Thailand, she said she had befriended a Chinese national, a school teacher, and that I was not to worry that she would be lonely or alone.'

'Do you know if her companion was male or female?'

'Yes, she said her name was 'Ming,' a woman.'

'This seems to confirm again that there were only women on the flight.'

The brother of the Tasmanian missing woman asked,

'Won't the airline provide the details on this?'

'That information has not come to us yet, there's a lot of red-tape to get through because this was not a commercial flight.'

'Has this not become an international crisis now? Why should red-tape prevent the release of this information? It's clear they disappeared once they boarded that wretched flight?'

'The concern is growing that this is a covert operation. Trickles of information are surfacing as families and associates realise that colleagues, friends and loved ones are unreachable.'

The representative from North Queensland, a man who appeared to be in his early sixties, studied each face in the room before he spoke.

'I am a concerned work colleague and have sketchy details on what this training involved. Do we know where this mission was operating from?'

'We have no information on that yet, either, it appears to be have been a water-tight arrangement.'

A male investigating officer added,

'We have set up a hotline, we need all your telephone numbers and suggest that it's imperative that you share your contact details with each other. At this stage, you are the only people who have come forth with your concerns. We are unsure if more Australian women are involved.'

Each member of the two groups was handed a journal to record any information they remembered about the days leading up to the departure of the missing women.

They were awkward with starting up a conversation with each other. Soon they began exchanging telephone numbers and shared their fears and hopes.

The female officer made the final announcement.

'We advise that none of you leave the country without letting us know your whereabouts at least forty-eight hours before, please.'

They stepped out with a slow funereal gait. Their faces were a contortion of concern — not knowing was a living hell.

8

RUMBLINGS

As the days passed, isolated from the world, where everything was handed on a platter, did nothing to subdue young Alva, a Swedish woman in her early twenties. She was restless, agitated and unhappy.

She spoke with no censorship.

'We have been duped, every one of us, you are blinded by the holiday atmosphere in here. Fair enough it's like being on a luxury cruise-liner, but come on, this is not life! Three months is a long time.'

Akanya piped in, in her customary motherly way.

'You do need to calm down. There is nothing else we can do, right now. Write a letter to your family, at least we have that option, you know. That tells me, we have not really been duped. Think of the higher purpose you will serve, once this time is over, right.'

'With due respect to you, Akanya, I don't agree that we have *not* been really duped. I'm inclined to agree with Alva, this is not normal, what we had at home is normal. We are not allowed to speak to our families and friends. Who writes letters these days? They don't check the mailbox at my place.' Audra said.

'Look, I get what you both are saying, but what is the sense in complaining, just get on with it and time will pass quickly enough.' Akanya added.

'No, no, we need answers from Masuyo. I am going to ask more questions about why we are trapped indoors.' Alva said.

Patience and Ming listened until Patience spoke up.

'We have every right to question the situation if we are unhappy, but let us keep our souls intact. Once we lose that, then we become victims of a situation that I believe has no intention of victimising us.'

'Geez, you say that with conviction Patience, almost like you are from the institution. On that note, who do we trust?' Audra added with raised, sneering eyebrows.

'We are entitled to our opinions, but I refuse to be negative.' Patience stated.

Patience studied the events timetabled each day, 'Purposefulness' 'Living in Your Truth,' 'Educating,' 'Coping with Separation' and 'Leading with Fire.' She studied the last event, the description was scant, *Let Passion Lead You to Lead Others. Without Fire There is No Light, No Hope.*' That particular event required mandatory attendance. The purpose seemed vague, she knew she had to seek clarification on that in the next Q & A session, which was scheduled once a week on a Friday. She pulled out the writing paper from the coffee table drawer and sat down to write Grace a letter.

Dearest Sis, you must be beside yourself now, concerned about my whereabouts and perhaps having thoughts that I might be dead. I am well on this day, I don't know when this will get to you. Let me assure you there is nothing to worry about, the undercover operation here has a higher purpose, it's not illegal nor sinister in any way. I am safe, but truth be told, I am not sure of my actual location, except to say I feel I am on board a luxury ship. I will write to you as often as possible, look after yourself. I will tell you more as my days here become clear to me. Trust I am safe and well. Love always, Patience xxx

DURING THE MORNING 'PURPOSEFULNESS' session Patience had a hasty note slipped to her by Zuri, who then disappeared out the back entrance. It was an invitation to meet privately with Masuyo. Everybody was seated in the auditorium in luxurious seats covered in a deep red, crushed-velvet fabric. Large gold light-fittings adorned both left and right walls. Everyone was dressed in pale grey tracksuits. Alexis, stood up at the podium, her blaze of red hair framed her small, freckled face. Masuyo was absent.

'Good morning ladies, this morning's session will clarify our mission to ourselves and others. I want you to feel comfortable, sit back in your seats, letting go of the tension in your neck, shoulders, wrists, knees and ankles.'

Alexis had a deep, strong voice, gentle eyes, and a permanent half-smile. Her Irish accent was easy on the ear. As she was about to highlight the mission's purpose, Audra raised her hand.

'Yes Ms Audra, do you have a question? I suggest holding the thought until the end of the session.'

Audra paid no attention to Alexis' request.

'What's happened to Alva? I heard she got ill last night. She's not here this morning.'

'Yes, Ms Alva took ill last night and is currently resting in the sanatorium. She will return to us as soon as she's well.'

A shuffling of feet and turning of heads towards Audra gave her the attention she craved. She stood up.

'Are we allowed to visit her after this session? What's really wrong with her? She seemed fine when I last saw her.'

'I am sure Ms Alva will appreciate your concern. It's best she is not disturbed by visitors at this stage. She needs to rest, away from the stress and anxiety she is feeling.' Alexis responded with a calm, ever-present half-smile.

'Is she medicated?' Audra persisted.

'No, Ms Audra, just resting. Shall we proceed with the session?'

The women settled in their seats again, Patience glanced around the room, feeling uneasy that the women seemed to be affected by Audra's concern regarding Alva. She sensed the agitation might be the fear that they too might succumb to the same fate as Alva. She forced herself to ignore the invasive thought. She had become a keen observer of the people and environment around her, uncertainty made her wary.

Alexis took them through the mission's values, emphasising that at the heart of purpose for self and others, the core values had to be summoned and lived.

'You must wake up each day with a distinct purpose. Write it down and fulfil it that day. Close your day with a blessed thought of thankfulness that you walked in your truth, lived compassion, and opened to understanding. Your final thought should be on what you did to lead another.'

Audra's under-her-breath comment reached a few ears.

'All I have on my mind when I get to bed is sleep, blissful sleep, my job is exhausting enough!'

Alexis looked up when she heard the soft laughter emanate from Audra's row of ladies. Akanya frowned at Audra's attention-seeking behaviour. Ming who sat two seats to the right of Patience, leaned forward to look at her. She had become dependent on knowing how situations were perceived by Patience. They exchanged a nod that a private conversation was necessary at some point that day.

Alexis continued to provide examples of purposefulness through nature and the recurring pattern of seasons, and the cycle of life. She led into how purpose empowers, guides and creates reactions, and directions for the next level of a defined, purposeful existence. A few nods around the room, and stilted silence made Patience aware that resistance lurked in this global city of women. She pondered how the selection process was initiated, why specific women were chosen, whether there was more than one delegate per country. Much was left to be answered. She supported the values, but she had to study Masuyo's actions if she hoped to be sure that her choice was a worthwhile one.

Xandria addressed the ladies on the order of the day, light refreshments were on offer in the greenhouse, the mini supermarket was closed for restocking and would open later that day. Two doctors were available when illness struck. Alexis was to be contacted if anyone felt ill. Mail was scheduled to leave on Wednesdays. The gym was open for a cardio class with Zuri, in an hour, or alternately ladies could go swimming in the aquatic centre. The movie theatre was available for selected screenings. The rostered lifestyle left little room for private, personal pondering.

Ming and Patience seized the invitation for refreshments in the greenhouse as their stolen time for a necessary conversation.

'What do you make of Alva's situation? Do you think she was silenced in being placed in the sanatorium?' Ming asked.

'I think she was stressed and perhaps needed a break away from the routine, to 'repurpose' her thinking. You must admit it's like being on a hamster wheel in here, it does not stop with all these timetabled activities. I had no idea Alva was ill until Audra mentioned it, did you?'

'To be honest, I heard raised voices, late last night, but stayed in my room, thinking it might be a few women having a difference of opinion.'

'Well, I heard nothing. I wish we had some sunshine, this artificial lighting might do my head in, and I might need time in the sanatorium too!' Patience laughed.

'Don't make light of this. Oh dear, that pun was not intended,' Ming was quick to ensure that what she said was not misinterpreted, 'we need to be aware that we might be altered after these three months. I'm not sure if I should say this, I found a note that was shoved under my door, inviting me to a meeting with Masuyo at four o' clock this afternoon.'

'I was not sure if I could tell you, but I received one too, my meeting is at two o' clock today. I can't imagine what it is about, other than that we are her chosen ones. Let's hope it's not too serious and that we can ask a few questions.'

Ming was relieved that Patience had a meeting with Masuyo. She disliked secrets and knew that she could trust Patience.

Patience wanted to know if there were more people residing in the mission building that they had not met yet, she intended knowing what else was in store for them. The 'artificial natural' surroundings with evergreen plants and shrubs seemed to calm the restlessness that arose that morning.

9

REDEFINING PURPOSE

Patience anticipated getting all her questions answered when she had her audience with Masuyo without the distractions that Audra was likely to cause, or Akanya's maternal chastisements about being grateful for being chosen to serve a higher purpose. What purpose, she questioned, when nothing had been clearly defined? What were they really expected to do on this mission as chosen ones?

Masuyo greeted Patience with a reverential bow, meeting her at the doorway to her ornate suite. A giant, wall-size collage of Rosa Parkes, Winnie Mandela, Eleanor Roosevelt, Nawaal el-Saadawi, and a host of other advocates on women's matters loomed in the room. A pale blue kimono with a vivid landscape of sky and rolling fields draped her small frame. She was calm, yet Patience felt something was hidden beneath her tranquil veneer.

This was Patience's first close-up meeting with Masuyo. As she bowed in return, she heard Masuyo say, 'Truth, Understanding and Compassion Greetings. Welcome.' Her voice was whisper soft.

Patience lit up any encounter with her exuberance.

'TUC to you too, Masuyo. Wow, your kimono is beautiful! Do we all get one?'

Masuyo smiled, 'it can be arranged if you like it. Let me get to the reason I asked for this meeting, as you have a busy schedule ahead of you, as do I.' She cut to her purpose, avoiding being over friendly.

'Yes, I am curious, so let's hear it. You seem to know everything about me. I would like to know more about you.'

Patience's unmistakable direct manner was her authentic, no veneer, no fluff, self. Masuyo studied her face, pondering whether this was her general stance in her interactions with others. She liked this attitude in Patience, there was an open frankness about her that invited a response.

'In my first meeting, I indicated that you all were chosen for the work you selflessly do for troubled women. You, Patience, were chosen for a bigger mission. We have studied your character, know about the situation when you were accosted in your home, how you reacted and proceeded with what you had to do. Your resilience and ability to dig into the matters affecting women's safety and advancement speaks to the heart of our mission. I have a few suggestions and would like to sound out your acceptance or rejection of what I have to say. Do you have any questions at this stage?'

'No, but I prefer to say, 'women in distress,' somehow, the word 'troubled' has connotations that the women are at fault. Just me feeling this way, I don't mean for you to change this. As for questions, I need more information, to formulate my questions in the right direction.'

Masuyo's steady gaze remained unaltered which fascinated Patience who knew, if someone plagued her with brash questions, she would be uncomfortable. She felt the urge to tap into this enigmatic captain of the aircraft, and commander of the organisation that brought her to this unknown place on a mission that was yet to be definitively clarified.

Patience's thoughts bounced around on the expanse of the mission's influence in extracting details on their private lives. Masuyo could not possibly know about the abduction in South Africa and temporary imprisonment at the chief's headquarters. She wriggled in her seat, itching to ask if there was a surveillance camera watching her in Australia.

'Firstly,' Masuyo's penetrating gaze was difficult to ignore. Patience looked at her, trying not to blink too much, as she waited to hear why she was summoned.

'You know you are here because we believe that you will have a global reach on rectifying the ills women, more particularly young women, face today. There is a plan that I will outline for you at the end of this session. The task at hand for immediate implementation, is that I want you to develop our third value among the women here, as in Compassion — this can be achieved through our 'Unveil Me' sessions in which women will volunteer to share the life challenges that steered them to the work they are currently involved in, on the outside. I am asking you to head these sessions as a vehicle to extend the compassion in our women on this mission. You do not have to answer in the minute, you have twenty-four hours to think about it, to allow with planning. If you go ahead with it, we start the sessions in a week.'

Patience looked up at the wall behind Masuyo, the faces of the women on the collage seemed to be looking at her, commanding her for a response. She sighed, shook her head then slowing nodded her acceptance of the role as a facilitator for Compassion.

'Are you agreeing to head this initiative? There are no contracts to be signed here, we are sisters with a common purpose as your Sisters Helping Sisters Organisation has been doing in Australia. All I need is a verbal agreement from you, should you accept my offer.'

'Thank you, Masuyo, for your vote of confidence, Compassion sits high on my life agenda. I was blessed to have two mothers, both of whom I will honour for the rest of my days. Yes, I will lead this initiative. I believe I will grow from such an experience.'

'Thank you, Patience, I knew we made the right choice bringing you in. Do you have any questions?'

'I'm not sure if you will answer this question, it's about our location, are we going to be told where we are and whether we will interact with men while we are in here? This might seem unrelated to your purpose, I have a human need to know.'

'Fair enough, the location we are in, has to remain undisclosed for a while longer. On the human need to have men around, I can confirm, we do have male interactions through some of our virtual motivational and gym sessions. Will the men be physically present? Not in the short-term, is all I can offer now.'

'Thank you for your honesty, so male visitors will arrive at some point.'

'This is correct. There are people at this station that you have not met, and perhaps will not have any need to meet, such as our catering and medical staff.'

'Catering staff, I would love to meet, I have a passion for food, eating and cooking,' Patience laughed, 'the doctor, I hope I do not have the misfortune to need.'

'They are all female staff, Patience, I hope this does not disappoint you.' She tried to conceal the urge to smile.

'Are you able to tell me what the other request is, that you saved to the end?'

'Once three months of our in-house training is over, we want to know if you are prepared to commit to another three, or perhaps six months, serving and educating women to become tomorrow's leaders? This is classified information, we do not want to unsettle the women who are having adjustment issues right now. I ask that you keep this request to yourself. It will not be offered across the board, and we might solicit advice from you, to help us select women for specific destinations.'

'I need my twenty-four hours to think on that Masuyo. I will get back to you. Will I know the destination before I agree? How is this classified information? It was mentioned at our introductory meeting. I want to be clear that this is a known aspect of this mission.'

'Classified in the sense that you have been asked to commit for a longer period. You can take all the time you need to decide, and the destination will be transparent to prepare you, should you take up the offer, that is.'

Patience stared at the floor, deep in thought, she had much to consider before agreeing to anything that extended her time away from her SHSO.

'Once you commit, you will know two weeks before you leave, where you will be sent to. Towards the latter half of your three months, I will address this in a meeting with all selected members, for feedback and suggestions on what everybody thinks about such placements.'

'There is still an air of mystery, I am not concerned, but know some of my peers will be stressed by such a request.'

'We shall cross that bridge when we get to it, Patience. Do you have any further questions?'

Patience stood up, extended her arm for a handshake.

'Perhaps later, I might have a few questions.'

Masuyo declined her hand, bowing low.

'May, Truth, Understanding and Compassion always light your way.'

Patience instinctively stepped backwards, with bowed head, she repeated, 'Truth, Understanding and Compassion, be with you sister.' When she reached the door, she turned around, leaving Masuyo standing in the room. Her fingers were loosely laced together, clasped close to her chest as if in prayer.

Patience headed back to her room, kicked off her shoes, sat on the edge of the bed with her head in her hands. Please guide me to the right decision, she thought. How would Grace react to the news that she might be away for another six months? How would she explain it? The offer was a tempting thought, but what if she was sent to a war-torn country? This was a real possibility. Was she ready to face new challenges that might threaten her safety in her mission to empower women? She knew the social and political landscape of Australia well — would she now have to brace herself with the strength of her former years in the chief's kraal? Grace would put her life on hold until she knew that Patience was safe. Could she sacrifice this bond with her only family? An image of Mama Varuna flashed before her. In the distance behind her, Mama Elsie's face glowed with pride.

She gathered her thoughts and left her room to continue with the rest of the program for the day. Ming suggested they take in a movie at the in-house theatre after dinner. She needed the distraction.

Later that evening they debriefed on their meetings with Masuyo. Ming, too, was asked to remain on the crusade after the three months of training ended. She was unsure if she would take up the opportunity, much depended on her teaching position, and whether a replacement would hold the fort for her, for another three, or perhaps six months.

Ming had a glow that Patience only saw after her meditation sessions. Being acknowledged, chosen to extend her service had added value to her world.

They were both two-thirds convinced they might accept the

task of addressing the challenges young women faced in countries that ignored the problem.

Patience connected with the purpose. Her own life took a different trajectory because Varuna Sharvin opened her doors to her and her mother, Elsie.

Convincing Grace that she had to do this, was a bridge she would cross later.

10

ANNOUNCEMENT

The following morning Alva was at breakfast, subdued, pale with dark circles around her eyes. What had happened to her in three days? She was as thin as someone surfacing from a famine. Akanya approached her.

'How are you Alva, are you feeling better, my dear? Is there anything I can do to help you?'

Alva made no eye contact, shook her head and continued to slowly guide a half-filled spoon of cooked oats into her reluctant mouth.

'You let me know if there is anything I can do, please.' Akanya touched her on the shoulder and walked away with concern written all over her face.

'Poor girl,' she said to Audra, 'I don't know if she's on medication, she seems to have lost her spark, you know.' Her head bobbed from side to side like a spring-loaded dancing doll.

'Who knows in here, she must be medicated, god knows who the doctors are in this place.'

'Alva was a little out of control, we must agree, I hope she feels well soon, perhaps she needs more rest.'

'Yes, I'm sure that would be good for her. I wonder what this unscheduled meeting with Masuyo is about, this morning. It must be for all the ladies if it's in the auditorium.'

'Hopefully, there will be some Q & A time fitted in, we must ask only pertinent questions, Audra, not to annoy anyone.'

'I just want to know when I can speak to my friends and colleagues. I can't write a letter they won't read.'

'My dear Audra, we must keep our emotions in check and learn to be patient.'

Akanya walked around chatting to everyone, checking if they had a good night and whether they enjoyed their breakfast. This set Patience pondering on whether Akanya had a private meeting with Masuyo too. Audra was aloof, a hard one to figure out, she was bold on some matters, but withdrawn on certain issues. Whether she was really committed to the mission occupied some of their thoughts. Akanya had eased herself into the 'one of them' status which any fool could see. There was an obvious need to be accepted which had Patience questioning what her life circumstances were.

MING CLUNG CLOSE to Patience in the auditorium, she was concerned that someone else might have fallen ill overnight. Audra walked over to them, a young woman with flaming red hair accompanied her.

'Hey, Patience did you know there is another delegate from your country here — this is Deidre from Tasmania. Deidre extended her hand to Patience.

'What do you know, the world's a small place when we don't know where we are, right?' Patience laughed, reaching out to encircle the young woman's hands with both her hands and an inclining of her head. African respect was still firmly implanted in her psyche after all these years. The visit to South Africa to connect with her mother's ancestors lit the remembrance of cultural values from her distant childhood.

'Lovely to meet you, Patience,' Deidre said, 'I believe we have another sister from South Australia here too, I haven't met her yet.'

'Isn't that interesting,' Audra added, 'I'm the only one from the United States, or so I've heard. Hell, but who knows, in here right?' Her booming laughter attracted attention for a fleeting second, then everyone went back to their conversations in their little groups. Audra was becoming known for her empty explosions.

'We should try to find our other Aussie sister, Deidre, and perhaps we might find more Australians here. We could have our own outpost at the mission, strength in numbers, I like that.' Patience winked and then laughed when she noticed Audra's raised eyebrow, the surprise written all over her face indicated she had missed the intended mirth.

Zuri stepped onto the platform and requested all to be seated.

Masuyo floated into the space, in her customary ethereal way. Her yellow flowing gown, billowed up behind her, inviting her celestial energy into the room.

'Good morning ladies, thank you for assembling so quickly. I apologise for giving you short notice, your activities for your rostered day will commence soon.'

Ming contorted her lips like Popeye with his pipe askew.

'I have a feeling she is going to mention that we are going to run the personal testimony sessions.'

'Don't worry, take each thing as it comes.'

Masuyo continued.

'There are a few changes coming up next week, a group of hairdressers will be in for the week, please make your bookings through Zuri and Alexis ASAP to avoid disappointment. Manicures and pedicures are available next week too. It's your pamper week. Patience, Ming and Akanya will be heading up the 'Unveil

Me' week in a host of sessions for you all to get to know each other on a more intimate level. Patience was aware that nobody reacted to that slipped in announcement.

Masuyo continued, 'and one more for next week, we have a Skype conference with an inspirational man, whose name won't be disclosed now. Four sessions will run throughout the day, be sure to book yourself in one of them. There will be a lucky draw on Thursday night to select the participants who will have control of the kitchen, with our hospitality staff, to unleash their cultural culinary skills. There was a euphoric applause on that announcement. Raucous cheers erupted, characteristic of that heard at sporting events, after a few beers had been consumed. Masuyo laughed, almost doubling over, enjoying the moment, for the first time, without restraint.

Audra raised her hand. Akanya was visibly flustered when she saw the American hand go up.

'May we ask a few questions now, Masuyo?'

'Yes, five minutes of question time is now open, so please be quick.'

'Well, I don't know how quick this can be, but, what are we being trained for? I know it's about women empowerment akin to our outside jobs, but what type of empowerment are we talking here?'

'Good question, Ms Audra,' Masuyo smiled, 'there's a quick answer to that question. We have one purpose, we are preparing young women to take on world leadership, making them capable of holding positions of Prime Ministers, Presidents, and any office of government around the world.'

'So no men in positions of power?' Audra asked.

'Yes, that's right. Five minutes of question time is now over! Have a pleasant day ladies.'

She abruptly floated out with the same ethereal aura. Zuri walked out behind her. Alexis slipped out through the door at the front of the auditorium.

Audra looked across at Akanya with frustration.

'This is political as I suspected, it is a positive move that will work well with TUC values, but I'm for balance, gender balance.'

'Everything in life is political, regardless of what we do, the mission is a good one. I'm just sorry I'm not twenty years younger, because being a head of state in my country, is an interesting prospect in the current climate.'

'On the contrary, Akanya, I don't intend to chase any such office, but will do my bit to promote the leadership of women.' Audra said.

'We are all already empowering women in our various outside enterprises, so that should not be an onerous task. What a TUC infused world it would be with only women leading the world.' Patience mused.

'Well in your country, it's about time you had an Aboriginal Prime Minister, we've done that in America, so when will Australia follow suit like you usually do?' Audra's look was audacious as one that demanded an answer.

'Good point, Audra, let's see if our delegate stationed there can bring that to pass.'

'You're very quiet Ming, how do these announcements sit with you?'

'I could use a haircut, a motivational talk, and would love to cook next week. I miss it.'

'Is that it? No thoughts on women running the world?' Audra insisted.

'I am empowering the girls I teach, to stand up and be counted, if they become world leaders that will make me very proud. I have no such intention for myself.'

'I see, I uphold that one has to support the self, first, in order to look after or extend a helping hand to others. Do you think we are really individuals or products of our societies?'

Ming studied Audra's body language, she had the ability to sense, with startling accuracy, whether people were authentic in what they asked or expected of others. As much as Audra made her uncomfortable at times, she knew that there had to be a good bone within her if she was chosen for this mission. Her calm, serenity guided her reaction.

'That makes perfect sense to me, Audra, we are individuals, making our choices in life, I believe, but, we are also 'products' of our close-knit worlds. Family and culture are more important than societal values for me.'

On that note, Audra was silenced. What could she have been thinking about those who did not concur with her vision of the role of self and others? Ming left the discussion to proceed to her next activity for the day.

Patience attended a session presented by Zuri. It intrigued her that someone as young as Zuri had words of wisdom on how to support women to advance in the world today. Ming attended Xandria's session on, *Authentic Lives*. Patience saw Akanya Das in the row in front of her, she was keen to observe her reactions to young Zuri's sharing of ideas on *Conscientising Friends and Family*. Patience perceived Zuri to be a lost soul, finding her way in an artificial world. She was curious to know more about the mysterious leaders under this vast dome structure that had all the luxuries of a grand ship.

11

AUTHENTIC LIVES

Soft, melodic singing bowl strains floated through sound system as Zuri set up her power-point, videos, and checked on the live streaming link from Quebec.

Everybody settled in their seats, fifty women were in attendance.

A calm Zuri, bowed her head as she said, 'Truth, Understanding and Compassion. Welcome, everyone.'

'In unison, fifty voices returned, 'Truth, Understanding and Compassion. Thank you, Zuri.' Patience felt the acceptance and compliance vibrating in the room. Everyone was eager to know more, to know what Zuri was going to offer.

'Thank you for signing up for my session. Today we will talk about how you should inform your friends and families on what your mission here has given you and the line of work you will enter into or extend, of course depending on what you're specifically doing in your careers on the outside. Firstly fill out the checklist on your family values. You will find it in the pocket of the seat in front of you.'

The inside of this conference room was like the inside of an aircraft, it was narrow and long, the seating was arranged alphabetically, no one took notice of it, filling up the seats as they arrived. A large screen on the front wall, and smaller screens at the back of each seat, equipped with headphones in each seat pocket, ensured everything was planned and executed with attention to detail.

The first power-point slide stated: Family and Friends, do they support your mission?

'How many of your families are aware of this mission you are on? Please raise your hands.'

Patience glanced around the room, with her hand up, there were only half a dozen others raised.

'Not many, so you are in the right session. Family and friends are your greatest allies to propel our mission forward. This is why awareness is vital. You must use your powers of persuasion to convert their thinking about our mission — men and women alike in your family, and social circle must be drawn into what you are working on.'

Photographs of happy families engaging in social justice initiatives flashed across the screen. Families, or friends serving at soup kitchens, working in classrooms, sitting outdoors in wonderment of nature, taking holidays with an educative purpose, by providing guidance to young women in museums, in their rural communities, in aged-care, and child-care facilities. Happy faces created a positive tone — young and old collaborating as mentors, guides, teachers, friends and role-models.

'Once you convince your people about the value of your work, you should invite them to participate in the work you're doing. You may well ask, how do you do this? You will be provided with online links to our mission before you leave, the visual has a greater impact these days than the spoken word alone.'

Akanya turned around to look at Patience with a raised eyebrow, impressed and bursting to ask questions, but she was forced to curb her tongue for a while longer.

A few short videos on women doing invaluable service played

in quick succession, designed to mesmerise and influence action. Patience gasped when she saw a photograph of herself with Felicity Cassano at the conference in Melbourne. How did they get access to the conference photographs? Could this mission be linked to an affiliate body in Australia? The world was no doubt a small place. Patience considered if attribution was given to the source, something Grace was pedantic about and ensured they adhered to in all matters of sharing ideas and resources.

The ladies eagerly awaited the treat of a live connection to the outside world. There was an unexpected ten minute break while Zuri ensured the live link was working. Refreshments were served with cheese, crackers and olives to go with a selection of wines and soft drinks. Patience met Akanya at the drinks table.

'Good to see you in action in that photograph. Did you provide it to the mission for use?' Akanya asked with a sly, half smile.

'Oh no, I was surprised when that came up. I wonder what else is not private anymore.'

'I see, yes indeed, we are almost celebrities with this access to our private lives, but celebrities with fame, not an income to match,' Akanya laughed.

'Celebrities? Would you trade this for that life?'

'It has been an untold desire from my teenage years to be a Bollywood star!' She laughed, embarrassed, when curious eyes looked at her from across the cheese platter.

'You can be anything you choose Akanya, that's the mission here.'

'What a thought, if only that was possible. My name in lights! Aaah, a dream!'

A bell sounded for a return to the room.

AFTER A FEW CRACKLING sounds from the gigantic speakers, a

booming male voice was heard.

'Hello chosen ones! Truth, Understanding, and Compassion. I am so happy to be invited to chat with you today!'

A few giggles and exclamations of, 'why hello there!' brought the house down in unrestrained laughter. The serenity established in previous weeks was forgotten. This male deprivation reaction confirmed that men were welcome in this environment. Just hearing a male voice engendered an air of flirtatious joyfulness.

'I am here as an ardent supporter of the mission. I will provide you with a my perspective on why a new age of leadership is essential for the world, in our very near futures. We cannot continue to be ravaged by testosterone driven wars! Women and children will not be sacrificed for the aggression and agendas they have not created. We have to move into the age of female leadership, we need Truth, Understanding and Compassion to rule, to define all our actions.'

He continued on for thirty minutes, highlighting the mission work that men were engaged in to conscientise communities that were steeped in patriarchal thinking.

At the end, he received a loud cheering with his Truth, Understanding and Compassion departure. He bowed before his voice and face faded out.

There was a glow on every face in the room. Akanya was relieved there was a male supporter of the mission. She was anxious about how she would take the message back to her country. She had hope, as did every bright-eyed and bushy-tailed woman at Zuri's session.

LATER THAT EVENING over a cup of green tea in Patience's room, Ming filled her in on her *Authentic Lives* session with Xandria.

'This session covered the value of authenticity in relation to race, culture, gender, education, and religion. Xandria said she deliberately left out class because the mission did not support class stratification. I suppose I should be used to that idea.' Ming smiled.

'Interesting on that last point, I would like to know more on how that is supposed to be achieved.'

'Yeah, globally that would take a seismic shift in values and ways of thinking. To sum up the overall session, it defined Truth as closely aligned with leading an authentic life. It stressed pride in race, culture, and gender. Religion was touched on in vague terms, and yet TUC values have religious overtones. Race and gender are significant areas, and I am overjoyed that this is being prioritised. Assimilation was denounced as trivialising the existence of cultures that were not rooted in western civilisation. I'm not sure how you will react when you hear this. Australia was listed as a case in point, and the disastrous effect this has had historically on Aboriginal communities. The Australian delegate from Queensland was in my group. I spoke to her during the break, she wants to meet you. I took it upon myself to tell her we could have breakfast together. I hope that's okay with you, Patience?'

'Thank you, I would love to meet her and have her in my personal testimonies session next week. I'm glad it was discussed, because even as a migrant in Australia I feel deeply about the marginalising of Aboriginal people as the traditional custodians of the land. My sister, Grace, says this significant aspect of Australian history is deeper than the apartheid system we were raised in. She finds taking a child away from its mother and family, barbaric, when the mother is not a criminal and has a proven record of love and care for her children. She feels this injustice with conviction and passion.'

'Your sister sounds like a person that this mission could use to good ends. Would she consider it, do you think?'

'Grace is not as daring as I am. She checks everything before she signs the dotted line, she might, but not before she has scrutinised the mission, its statement and of course, the leaders. A touch of the sceptic, a version of Audra, not in a crass way, more as an informed decision-maker. She won't be easily persuaded, and besides a love interest is on the horizon for her. By now it's probably well over the horizon! A doctor too, that she says is 'a lovely man'. I've met him, and he is a fine man.' Patience enjoyed talking about her sister, it made her feel Grace's presence.

'She has her head in the right place and her heart too. How did your session go with baby Zuri, was she any good?'

'Far from 'baby Zuri' I assure you, and I won't call her young or a baby after today, she ran an excellent session. She must have been well-trained by Masuyo and Xandria and whoever else trained this lot. She has wisdom beyond her years. It was quite inspiring.'

'She would have been a great student to have in a classroom, teacher's dream, I'm sure. So what was the highlight for you?'

'Girl, let me not get started on this! The deep-voiced man talking to us had me weak at the knees, girlfriend! You should have heard the womanly appreciation, it was quite something — deprivation is a dangerous thing.' Patience hunched over, laughing as she recalled that moment. How did your group react?'

'It was marvellous seeing and hearing a man supporting the mission's vision. The reaction was appreciative in my session with him, although not raucous. Was Audra in your group?'

'No, I'm not sure what she did during that session. Akanya was there and loved the male perspective. I could tell from the look on her face. Her country would benefit from outsider views on this, although male celebrities in India do have a call to action on respect for women.'

They chatted for another hour, speculating on what countries they might be offered to carry the mission forward after their days of training.

12

DECISIONS

Grace moped around the house and was subdued at work. She was grateful to have Andrew Lang as her second in charge in the ER facility at City Hospital. Friday nights had brought in many more injured persons in recent months, more victims of aggression. The increasing prevalence of easy access to guns in Sydney unnerved her. She bemoaned the loss of the gun-free society she migrated to, almost twenty years earlier. Late night brawls and cars hurtling into pedestrians had changed the social landscape.

Andrew brought her a cup of coffee and a biscuit to soothe her frayed nerves.

'Grace, you have to get some sleep, you can't go on like this. Remember, not having word might mean that Patience is not in danger, it is a difficult situation to be in, but your sister would want you to be strong through this.'

'Oh Andrew, I know, it's a tough one, we were both beginning to see the light in our lives, and now this curve ball has me in a spin. I'm seeing Dr Deakin again next week to help me cope with the anxiety. As you know, once you're clinically diagnosed with anxiety, stress factors can turn the tables. I can't go through that again.'

'Telling you to calm down is ludicrous when we are not going through the emotions that are playing out for you, with each day of no contact with Patience.'

'I'm in an added dilemma, Keefe wants us to go to Ireland, his mother has advancing lymphoma, that's a ticking situation — and not knowing Patience's situation has me in an emotional lockdown. I can't make any major personal decisions now. Keefe is keen to talk about marriage, that's a no-go zone if my sister is missing.'

'She loves you both, surely you must know that she will be happy with whatever decision you make in your relationship with Keefe.'

'I know, Andrew, but I can't commit to anything, least of all marriage, Patience is the only family I have.' She shook her head, looking at Andrew through misty eyes.

'I have to let Keefe know by Sunday if I will go with him to Ireland. He can't hang around waiting for me, I would never forgive myself if he missed seeing his mother alive.'

'You should go, Grace. You really should, you must meet Keefe's mother. You can keep abreast with what's going on with Patience from there. How long does Keefe plan to be away?' Andrew was happy for Grace, even though his heart spoke a different truth for the love he might have shared with her. He was concerned that this situation would set her back, after her recovery from her trauma in South Africa.

'Two weeks is all the time he can get right now. I will have a think about going. It's not sitting easy with me, I keep thinking, what if Patience turns up and I'm off in Ireland. What sort of sister will I be?'

'Dear God, Grace, you have to stop doing this to yourself. Patience will never judge you.'

'I know, I know. It's how I feel... I suppose we better get back on shift, a rough night awaits us. We have to brace ourselves for the avalanche that might hit us.'

Andrew watched her walk away, shoulders stooped, unsmiling and lethargic. Grace was losing the spark she regained a year ago. She was slipping into her old ways. He had to do everything in his power to keep her from sinking further into this melancholic state.

She was exhausted after her night shift, she sauntered to the carpark with Andrew, he gave her a peck on the cheek and tousled her hair like a little brother would.

'Be good Grace, I'll call you.'

'Thanks Andrew, I might call before you do, rest well.'

Keefe had the morning off, he tiptoed into Grace's apartment and shut her bedroom door to prepare breakfast without disturbing her. He held off with the juicer, afraid the pulsing sound would shock her out of her sleep. He was meticulous, almost surgical in how he trimmed and chopped the fruit — cut to precision, apple slices, ginger and oranges waited on the kitchen counter, ready to be juiced. He beat the eggs, sliced the mushroom and banana, and grated some cheese in preparation for an omelette, just the way Grace liked it. He sat down with his coffee, laptop open, earphones in, listening to the cool grooves of Carlos Santana, as he finished up a research paper he had been working on.

Grace rose at 10.30 am to the heady aroma of freshly ground, percolated coffee. She inhaled, stretched her arms like a content kitten, and bent down to reach her ankles — this was her waking up ritual. She was tempted to get a cup of coffee but rushed to the shower instead. Wrapped in a cotton gown, she strolled into the kitchen to meet Keefe.

'Look at you, busy-bee, when did you come in? I must have

been in a very deep sleep not to hear you. Sleepless nights finally caught up with me. I didn't hear you come in nor a sound coming from the kitchen!'

'That's good, I got in around nine o' clock. Here, sip on this juice, I pulsed the fruit when you went into the shower. I tried not to wake you with my domestic sounds!' He laughed, reaching out to hug Grace.

'Mmmm... you smell like a freshly powdered baby! Coffee is ready, have the juice first out on the balcony, it will be a spring clean of the innards after a hectic night. I'll be ready in a jiffy with your omelette and a serving of smoked salmon and smashed avocado, just like Dr Sharvin likes it. Go along now, the kitchen is out of bounds to you this morning!'

'I will, you are adorable Dr Daly, you look dashing in my mother's apron, and that accent is enough to make any girl swoon!' Sleep had worked wonders. Waking up to Keefe in the apartment was what she needed to lift her mood.

Breakfast was a treat. Keefe told her she looked like a satisfied kitten. Then a serious look crawled across his face, his voice dropped to a whisper.

'Grace, you know I want to spend the rest of my days with you. I want this every day. Have you given some thought to coming to Ireland with me to see my mother?'

Grace stopped sipping her coffee, not knowing how to respond without hurting his feelings. With her cup poised mid-air, at a precarious angle, she said nothing.

'What is it Grace? Why are you so quiet? Speak to me about what's going on in your head and heart? You can say 'no', you know, I understand... I won't be upset, I promise.'

She cleared her throat, sensing his need to know now. Her voice cracked, 'it's not that, so much has happened, I feel trapped. You know nothing will make me happier than knowing you will always be in my life.'

Now Keefe was silent. He cocked his head to the right in an

upward glance at her. He did this when he was serious or contemplating a decision.

'Now, you're scaring me, are you upset that I want to wait until Patience is back?'

'Not at all. I'm surprised that you are putting your life on hold when you have no concrete evidence of where she is or when she'll be back.'

'I miss my chats with my sister, Keefe. I want to talk to her about our relationship moving to the next level. I hope you understand.'

'I do, I know it must seem rushed, me talking about spending the rest of our lives together and...' He stopped for fear that his persistent talk of marriage, would shut her off, 'I appreciate that you would want to have a heart-to-heart with your sister. I hope you come to Belfast with me... I would love to have my mam meet you.'

'Being in your life for the rest of my days is what I cherish... asking you to wait is not fair. I promise to give you an answer by Friday, if not sooner, whether I can go to Belfast with you. I have a few things to check on, on the work front too.'

'You could have updates on Patience while we are in Belfast. Virginia and Andrew would also keep you updated. I can wait, Grace, I have waited my whole life, but will be praying that you will make this trip with me, at least.' He stood up, walked across to her and lifted her off her chair. He hugged her with a fierceness she had not felt from him before. She pulled away.

'What's this in your pocket?' She laughed, feeling anxious that Keefe was intense, that early in the day. She hated feeling out of control, always needing to be in charge of everything and everyone.

She had not expected the answer she got. He was not one to harbour secrets when asked any questions. He was direct, much like a schoolboy caught out on a plan he had. Keefe pulled out an engagement ring from his shirt pocket. He had come over to her place that morning with serious intent. She felt awful for dampening his expectation, ruining the moment he wanted to create. He held back on what could have been a precious moment, when she voiced her hesitation.

A beautiful vintage diamond ring gleamed up at her.

'It's my grandmother's, she left it to me to give to my future wife. My mother held off giving me the ring in my first marriage, there was something she said, about that marriage that did not sit well with her. And right she was, it did not sit well with me either, short and not sweet, but rather bitter it was. I will wait, Grace... I'm a patient man.'

Grace pressed her temples, she felt the pressure exploding in her head. She wanted more than anything to have Keefe forevermore in her life, but she could not make life decisions with Patience somewhere in limbo.

'What an ingrate you must find me, Keefe, I've just destroyed a beautiful moment for you. I would love to make that life-long commitment now if I could, but how can I at this moment...'

'I know this is a lot to ask now, but I'm happy to wait until Friday, before I book the tickets to Belfast. No expectations, but just to meet my mother, for her to see you, as I see you. You have not ruined the moment, you have not said no, I'm hopeful.' His eyes lingered on hers, his heart written all over the tenderness of that moment.

'Thank you,' was all she could say.

LATER THAT DAY Grace stopped off at Patience's place. She offered to assist Virginia Bale with walking Sprite and Ajax while Patience was away. They bounded into the house as soon as she opened the patio doors. Both clambered for a pat on the head.

'Calm down boys, too much excitement is not good! I know

you both miss Patience but give me a break, I will be taking you out now, but you must calm down!'

Virginia met her in the park outside the SHSO offices. Sprite and Ajax ran around, berserk, like two prisoners let loose upon seeing Virginia. They jumped up on her, licking her face in big wet, dribbling swoops. The force of their loving bodies caught her unawares, sending her tumbling to the ground.

'Oh dear, Virginia, are you hurt?'

'No, just happy to see these darling boys, what a treat to see them this early, thank you, Grace.'

'You're welcome, here,' she extended her arm, 'let me help you up. I promised my sister I would help out whenever I could, and besides it gets me outdoors, and lord knows I need the exercise!'

'Don't we all, look at me falling over?' Virginia laughed.

They chatted about Patience's whereabouts, praying she would return soon. Virginia found it difficult to call Grace, *Grace*, maintaining the formal, 'Dr Sharvin' address.

An uneasiness consumed them when Grace remembered that Felicity Cassano intended paying them a visit soon, to chat about an action plan for Patience's return.

Grace knew she would have to have all her ducks in a row before Felicity arrived.

13

A FRIEND IN NEED

Felicity arrived at two o' clock on Saturday afternoon. She arranged a carer for Alf. His health had declined in the months after their wedding. Grace caught a glimpse of her flustered arrival, she braced herself for a barrage of questions.

'Hello Grace, what a hectic departure, Alf's carer cancelled at the last minute, I had to ring in for a replacement. Needless to say, he's unhappy it's someone he's not familiar with. I have to leave on the first flight out tomorrow morning.'

Grace listened as she thought about how to react without upsetting Felicity.

'Thank you for flying over Felicity, we could have discussed the situation on the phone. Alf needs you.'

'Bah! Can't get much through telephone chats, they are as bad as emails. I need a coffee so let's grab one at the hotel.'

Grace didn't protest when Felicity called to tell her she would be staying in a city hotel, not to disturb any domestic arrangement she had with Keefe. As much as she wanted to protest that there was no such arrangement, she had learned the less said always worked well in her relationship with Felicity.

The traffic from the airport to the city was as dense as usual in Sydney.

'I hate the traffic here, Melbourne is hectic too, but the roads are well planned for ease of movement, whoever planned the freeway tunnel had no foresight about growth in this city.'

Grace heard this grumble every time Felicity came to Sydney.

'Yes, it gets worse with each year, more people and greater congestion.'

'How are things in your ER facility? How's your latest love interest? I've yet to meet him, will I see him this weekend?'

'ER is a busy place, congested as the freeway most nights, to be honest, far more aggression and injuries inflicted of late. Keefe is well, I could ask him to join us for drinks after dinner if you're up to it.'

'Yeah, yeah, should be fine, tell him to come over later. What's the latest on Patience?'

'No news, since we last chatted.'

'How does this happen in this day and age where aircrafts disappear without a trace? All the passengers it appears were only women, right?'

'It is baffling, the Australian government is delving in to find out more. Three Australian nationals, which includes Patience, have been identified as being on that flight to Thailand, at this stage. There could be more.'

'The mystery of it all, is that you don't know the details of the mission Patience was on. How is that possible? I thought you both knew everything about each other.'

Grace squirmed under this first attack, she knew she would be blamed for the loss of contact with Patience. Silence was an option, but given Felicity's level of agitation, she had to think through quickly how she responded.

'Patience was not forthcoming with the details of the mission. She was overjoyed to be chosen. With due respect, she is a responsible adult, I didn't want to pry into what she had already made up her mind about.'

'Come on, Grace, you can't be serious, not pry, you're sisters for Christ's sake! We have no idea where she is, whether she is alive or dead!' For the first time in all of the sixteen years that Grace knew Felicity, it was the first time she heard, amidst her anger, intense fear that tested her sensibilities, cracking her voice in mid-sentence. She was confused, irate, and stressed. Grace remained calm — Patience and Felicity shared a bond that did not include her on some matters.

'There is an action group set up and more is being done to unveil this mystery. Families of the missing women, globally have come forward, there's an active response Facebook group set up, but at this point, we're all unsure where to meet in the world.'

'Have the aviation officials in Bangkok made any comment yet, on why the aircraft did not arrive as scheduled?'

'Nothing from them yet, but Canberra reports that they have no record of the plane leaving Singapore, that is where the current location becomes confounded.'

'With sophisticated technology at their disposal, you mean to tell me, they have no inkling if it even left Singapore!'

Question after question, left Grace no room to offer thoughts on her speculations until she squeezed in, 'Patience sent me a message that she was boarding the flight to Bangkok from Singapore, and that she had met a Chinese national on the same mission.'

'That is useless information if we don't know if she left Singapore at all.'

'The Canberra action group has information, from a source that does not want to be named, that the flight left as scheduled, and that contact was lost forty-five minutes into flying time. That's where the mystery comes in. Why can't the Singapore source be named? Who is being protected? My concern is not the political agenda, all I want to know is whether Patience is safe, wherever she is.'

'Most often as history will attest, missing planes are never recovered intact, debris is usually found in places the aircraft was not scheduled to fly over. How much longer do we wait?'

'I'm sorry Felicity, I'm as much in the dark as you are, but I have hope, that is what I want to hang onto.'

'As we all do. What time is Patience's assistant meeting us? Perhaps she can shed more light on what Patience was thinking when she accepted this bizarre offer.'

All Grace wanted to do was to get back home to bed, to avoid Felicity's insensitive comments. She detested the dismissive reference to Virginia as 'Patience's assistant.'

Virginia arrived at 7 pm. Her nervousness was obvious, she fiddled with her hair, twirling the ends into a messy, matted knot, avoiding eye contact with Felicity. Grace tried to protect her from Felicity's interrogation. It was as if they were on trial for what happened. Felicity wanted the nitty-gritty on what Patience said about the mission she was embarking on, she wanted answers on whether either of them tried to stop her, or asked questions neither of them had any answers to.

'Patience spoke to me two weeks before she left,' Virginia explained, 'she was overjoyed that an international human rights cooperation had chosen her to join their conference in an all-expenses paid trip. She said the skills she would gain would bring our SHSO up to world standard. I jokingly told her that I hope they selected me for their next round, and that she should tell them about me. We both laughed about how powerful we would be as a joint force in our mission to protect abused women in Australia.'

'So there is another mission, how much do you know about this?'

'Oh no, that was just me speculating about more missions like this in the future.'

The questions were fast and furious, and each one made Virginia and Grace feel increasingly guilty and responsible for not being more informed on Patience's mission.

Keefe joined the ladies for drinks around nine-thirty that evening. Felicity was cordial for the first few minutes before her tongue got the better of her.

'You sure know how to scout out a good-looking man Grace! Especially after your breakdown in Melbourne last year. I might need to see Dr Deakin myself soon with the way my life is going!' She threw her head back and laughed like a snake-haired Gorgon.

Grace's ears burned, her cheeks were aflame. She shot a glance at Virginia who idolised her. Virginia sat with lowered eyes, terrified to breathe. Keefe raised his glass and announced,

'Here's to finding Patience safe and sound, Grace has all the support she needs and more to ensure that this happens.'

'You're cock-sure about that Keefe, what do you know that we might not know?' Felicity asked with a frown.

'My insider information tells me that Patience, from our few engagements, is a woman with her head screwed on the right way. She would not take on something if she had any inkling that it would jeopardise her safety or her life for that matter. I believe she is tucked away, upping her skills and will return when the mission is accomplished.'

'Wow, so are we expected to just sit around and wait for that day, some day in the future, ten, twenty years from now?'

'Not at all Felicity, I'm not suggesting that. Grace will be involved in providing any missing links that she might remember as will Virginia, but we are hopeful Patience will return, soon. She said three months, I doubt it will be twenty years.' He looked Felicity square in the eye as he spoke his truth.

'That is my hope too, but I'm not one to sit around waiting, Grace will allow me to make my own inquiries.'

'Any inquiry will be good and yes go ahead, do you have an immediate plan we can assist with?' Grace asked.

'I'm thinking of flying to Singapore to the site where the aircraft was last seen, and I will question authorities there.'

'How will you do that, with Alf being unwell? Please don't do anything in haste,' Grace cautioned.

'I will arrange for his care, don't worry yourself over that. You have contacts in The Netherlands, we should tap into The Hague getting involved. Can you speak to your contact there?'

'Nina Holstead? Yes, I could, but, I'm not sure what she can do. Keefe knows her husband too.'

'Well, what are we waiting for? We need to tap into all our contacts locally and internationally if we hope to have Patience back home.'

Virginia was silent throughout Keefe's discussion, she looked up with emotion brimming in her blue eyes.

'She will return soon, Felicity. We have to believe that.'

14

—————

I AM AKANYA

Patience had a restless night, in the days leading up to her 'Unveil Me,' sessions. She contemplated whether she should kick off the session with her own South African trauma. She spoke to Ming and they agreed that it was not a good idea to begin the sessions with their personal stories, perhaps they could end the session with it or go over as a guest to each other's sessions and present their story. They decided to ask Akanya if she thought it was a good idea.

'Why? I don't understand, why is it not proper to begin with your own personal story? I don't have a problem with doing that.'

'Fair enough Akanya, you go ahead with it as you want, Ming and I will swap for the first session and address our group. We don't mean to impose on how you want to run your sessions.'

'Let me think about it, I will let you know tomorrow, it's not that I'm completely closed to the idea.'

Patience found Akanya difficult to understand, it was almost as if after being resistant, she was going to do it. Her hand gestures where elaborate when she said, 'completely.' The circular motion of both her hands, from her chest outwards suggested that waiting until morning was essential to her decision. She looked at them, shook her head in her customary swivel-bobbing-head motion, then said, 'Don't worry, everything will be okay, just keep calm.' The circular hand gesture that accompanied, 'everything' made Ming smile.

'Thank you Akanya, see you in the morning. Sweet dreams,' Ming said.

'Haaa, sweet dreams? No such thing in here, but I will chant before I sleep, that keeps me calm.'

Patience avoided eye-contact with Ming who was about to burst into a fit of giggles.

'She means well, Ming, we have to appreciate her for that, we all have our eccentricities.' Patience could not help herself imitating Akanya's circular hand gesture when she said, 'all' which set them off laughing like two crazy school girls.

'Stop it Patience, being in here without excitement or entertainment, will have us doing that all the time without realising it.'

'Yes, I agree, but a little bit of healthy laughter, as long as it does not harm anyone, is good. Inside joke, girlfriend!'

'Goodnight Patience, Truth, Understanding and Compassion, and sweet dreams to you.'

'And you, my friend.'

DAY ONE OF THE 'UNVEIL ME' sessions began. Patience was very pleased that Akanya was to be her first speaker. She would speak to her group in the latter half of the week.

Akanya's black hair was left hanging loosely about her shoulders, not in her usual tightly plaited, pinned bun at the back of her head. She wore a white kaftan which gave her a ghostly look, her expression was serious. With downcast eyes she walked to the podium. She looked up at the eager faces before her, and closed her eyes in obvious silent prayer before she began.

'Greetings one and all. May Truth, Understanding and

Compassion prevail? I have been lovingly invited to share my personal world with you to shed understanding on why I chose this path of selfless service. I was born fifty-five years ago into a rural family, in a remote village in Panna in Madhya Pradesh. My parents had toiled the land for many years and were physically older than they were in years, from the hard work they endured, to feed us, their children. I am one of two daughters, my baby brother died two days after his birth. My mother was unable to breastfeed him and my father did not have the money for powdered baby milk. They fed him cow's milk which caused severe dysentery leading to his death.

There were no formal schools in my childhood days, whenever my aunt visited us from Delhi, which was only once a year, she brought all the books and pencils she could carry for my sister and I to read and write. Both my parents did not speak English, so for at least the first ten years of my life, I spoke the vernacular with no exposure to English until I was a teenager. I was raised in a very poor family, but we were rich in love and respect for each other.'

She looked up at the group, some had tears in their eyes and others could not look her in the eye.

She continued, 'there were no egos and worship took precedence, at sunrise and sunset. Out of one plate of food, cooked on an open fire, largely consisting of steamed rice and a few potatoes, we ate just enough to sustain us.'

In a bid to lighten the mood that crept over the room, she added, 'you must wonder how I got so rotund then,' her hands did its usual circular swoop to depict what she understood to be 'rotund.' A faint murmur rolled around the audience.

'Things became difficult when my father passed away, my mother was expected to be available for the needs of widowers in the village. She hated being violated this way and gave birth to a baby boy who she could not look at, nor raise. My younger sister and I raised Biddhu from infancy. My mother passed away six months after his birth. I believe she died from the stress and shame she had to bear for the demands placed on her, as a widow. I don't want you to feel sad, just open your eyes to what life is for women in countries outside your own.'

Patience felt overwhelming dread as she anticipated worse to come.

'One night as my sister and I lay asleep with Biddhu, we heard the sound of horses approaching, we peered out our little mud house. The fields around us were torched, flames rose in crackling anger. A group of men barged into our tiny home and had their way with us. They left us for dead, bleeding, writhing in pain, and rode off before morning broke. My sister, Meena, died the next morning. Her internal injuries were severe. She was a little one, these men were brutal.'

A sob broke out at the back of the room, two women walked out to comfort the young, sobbing woman. Something triggered the emotion in the core of her soul. Patience sat in numb silence as her heart pounded with emotion and memory of days gone by. Akanya paused, waiting for everyone to settle after the young woman was taken outside, and continued.

'One kindly woman came to Biddhu and I, she washed us, fed us and kept us in her house. Three days later authorities took us to a foster home in Delhi. Biddhu was adopted very soon by a wealthy family. I was older and left without a family that wanted me. I have not seen Biddhu since the day he was taken away — I am sorry if my story distresses you, but there is a positive outcome for me. I stayed on at the home and became a carer to the new children coming in.

A nun who was living at the home at the time taught me to read and write in English. Later she helped me set up a shelter for women who were shamed by deeds they did not encourage nor perpetrate. I am a living example of survival after trauma. My body tells a different story with scars and burns, but by God's grace, I am alive. Thank you for listening and I am happy to answer any questions in the days ahead.' She put her hands together, bowing low, whispering, 'Truth, Understanding and Compassion be with you, always, sisters.'

The women walked up to Akanya, some hugged her, sobbed on her shoulder, and others thanked her for sharing what was a painful experience to recount.

Patience saw an outpouring of compassion like she had never seen since her mother's and Mama Varuna's profound display of affection for her and Grace. She was amazed at Akanya's lack of bitterness, humility and dedicated service to others. Had Akanya not shared her story, she knew she would have judged her as a 'bossy' woman who wanted to be the annoying 'mother' to everyone. Her lesson that day was that one never knows someone until one has heard their story. She was filled with a deepened respect for Akanya, wise Akanya who told everyone to remain calm, and to be grateful for being chosen on this mission.

Audra sat in her seat, sobbing, unable to walk up to Akanya. Patience went to her, she was inconsolable.

'Come, walk with me a while Audra, you need a change of scene.'

Audra rose like a docile puppy, all sense of the need to argue, washed away.

'That is one phenomenal woman, Patience, how could I have judged her, how could I?' she sobbed afresh, hurt by her own lack of sensitivity.

'We all did, Audra, it's why we're here, to break those walls of judgement to make us better at what we do.'

'May I please share my personal story in your session tomorrow, Patience?'

'Certainly Audra, that makes me happy to have you volunteer to do this.'

Masuyo asked to see Patience to discuss how the first session went. Zuri told her that Akanya's story had moved everyone in the room.

Patience was silent for a while before she said, 'I see the reason why you included this sharing session, but know that there is much more that will be heard that will never be forgotten. Akanya was very brave in her recount, she told her story with honesty and no self-pity. She is indeed a remarkable woman.'

'That is why we chose her, like you and the others, Patience. Always remember that you are all remarkable women. Empathy, the mother of compassion, is elicited through collective sharing of human memory, and experience. Separation and suffering is everyone's experience, they create our universal connectedness, not war and brutality triggered by inhumanity.'

She bowed, her face hard and unsmiling as she left with TUC on her lips.

Akanya's story was a brutal one, and yet it was a softening reminder of their purpose, here at the mission.

15

AUDRA'S STORY

Patience reasoned over and over again why the confessional sessions were necessary. She understood the mission's choice to include them. What she was unsure of was whether this was the mission's norm, or had Masuyo added it in on a whim?

The outpouring of understanding and compassion were self-evident after Akanya's testimony. She cringed for the hundredth time that she cast a critical eye on Akanya's attitude to life. She did indeed have so much to be thankful for. Masuyo wanted strong women to exalt the mission's cause. Patience was elated by the thought that she was on the cusp of a new era. To her it appeared to be a merging of social and religious values with a dash of political thinking. She sighed, what a time to be living in, to be involved in history in the making! For all life had thrown at her, she was blissful, unmarred, she had a chosen purpose, guided by an unseeing hand. She was motionless, absorbing the overwhelming feeling spreading through her body, leaving her light, winged — she gave silent thanks for the mothers that graced her life.

THE WOMEN GATHERED in the meeting centre, early the next morning — unsure and nervous that what might be revealed that day could possibly unlock their own vulnerabilities. The telling of personal stories had the power of creating emotional connections.

Zuri welcomed everyone with her youthful freshness. Her glow was unmistakable, clad in a pale-blue tracksuit, she was the picture of good health, a placid soul whose serenity was remarkable for one so young.

Alexis and Akanya attended Patience's sessions in this larger venue. Xandria assisted Ming with her smaller group.

AUDRA STEPPED up to the microphone. Her flushed face and trembling hands a far cry from the bold, brazen Audra they had come to know, she was transformed.

'Hello everyone, Truth, Understanding and Compassion be with you. Please don't pity me, I want you to hear me, understand and take what you can to empower young women to handle life with foresight and inner strength, both that I sadly lacked. Am I responsible for the slings and arrows of my life? I leave you to decide, once you have heard my story. With all the years that have passed, I am still my worst critic — the memory is suppressed, but never dies.'

A faint shuffling of awkward feet suggested that Audra had her audience in the palm of her hand, ready and anxious to hear her revelation. No whispers, just eager wide eyes fixed on her face.

'I was born Sophia, in Louisiana, fifty years ago, born with a silver spoon to prosperous parents. I wanted for nothing as an only child. My mother was a high flying socialite, my father a Wall Street giant. So what could go wrong?'

A cough in the back row, a hint that someone was beginning to feel uncomfortable, perhaps a familiarity was being born.

'My parents lived in New York, I lived in the family home in Louisiana, with Catena — my mother brought her distant cousin from Sicily to be my nanny. Rich and spoilt? You got that right! I was a brat! Poor Catena, I loved her but did not take her advice on anything. I was the madam of the manor!'

The audience laughed as Audra broke the ice, letting them into her world.

'At fifteen I met and had a fixation on the new boy in my school, Ramón Lopez. He too was a kid of wealthy parents who sent him to school in Louisiana with his nanny, his mother's sister, Romina, a woman I adored. His parents ran their business in Mexico. Ramón was lean, handsome, his rush of black hair and dark eyes with the sun shining through his locks, had my heart strings in a knot from the first day we walked home from school. He lived on the next street from me, a new gorgeous kid, needing a friend. If you thought Danny Zuko from *Grease* was a catch, you would have thought you died and went to boy heaven if you met my Ramón. Oh yes, he was mine, I possessed him, mind, body, and spirit. I had never felt as loved as I did then.'

Appreciative murmurs and Danny Zuko's name was whispered with glee, creating a momentary relaxed mood.

'My parents were too busy to notice my romantic inclinations. Catena warned me to stay away, I remember her words, I can still almost hear them, 'Sophia, this new boy, you must be careful, we don't know his family, get to know more about him, you must stop seeing him every evening, please Sophia.' I paid no attention to her cautionary words. I was in control of my own heart. I spent all my nights and weekends at Ramón's house. My school grades dropped — my parents did not ask nor show any interest in my academic achievements, or more the lack of it. I started smoking weed, doing everything that no parent would want their child to be involved in. Careless and carefree was my motto.'

Patience looked at the audience and back at Audra — she felt choked as memories flooded back of Mama Varuna and Elsie as God-given mothers. She shivered thinking what if she had not had them to guide her. She listened, hanging onto every word Audra uttered.

'One day, Ramón found Romina crying in the kitchen, he discovered that his mother was very ill. This news changed the course of both our lives. We left by road for Mexico, at dawn the next morning. Romina begged Ramón not to go, his last words to her as he sobbed, ring in my head to this day, 'she's *mi madre;* I am *su hijo.* How can I not go to her?' I had never thought of myself this way, as the daughter of my mother. I was an outlier, non-existent to my parents, I yearned for this connection Ramón had. We had a long drive ahead of us, I would do whatever it took to go with him to his mother. Ramón was seventeen at the time, an unregistered driver in a hired car that we coerced, the soft-hearted Romina to sign for. We stopped off in Corpus Christi for the night, I couldn't drive, Ramón was an inexperienced driver and fatigue got the better of him. We attracted suspicion when we stopped to refuel in Houston City, the filling station manager asked to see Ramón's driver's licence. He said it was in the car and drove off leaving the money on the bowser.

We arrived, aware of the dangers as we approached Mexico City, Ramón abandoned the hired car before we got to the border checkpoint. We travelled the rest of the way on foot until we reached the city. It was one-thirty in the morning — not the best time to be on any city street. Ramón said we had to walk to a particular location where his childhood friend would meet us. Out of nowhere, we heard a voice call out, 'Ramón Lopez, finally!' Ramón told me to run, pushing me away from him — three gunshots rang past me. Ramón fell to the ground with a heavy thud. I rushed up to him, I did not see who shot him, he was covered in blood and dust, he lay still — I knew he was dead.' There was a loud gasp from the audience who had been sitting tense and attentive. 'I ran back in the direction we came from, not knowing where I was, not sure where I was running to. A car screeched up beside me, a burly man grabbed me, threw me in the backseat of what looked like a Chevy. I was gagged, not sure where I was on this ride to hell. I have no recollection of when I was thrown out of the car. I woke up on the side of the road, somewhere. I had no time to process Ramón's horrific murder — I had to find my way home. My bags were in the hired car, I had no money on me. Rich Louisiana girl with not a cent in my hand! If ever, there was a life lesson of heartache, loss, and poverty, I had them all at the same time. I hitch-hiked my way back home, I was given a ride from one town to the next by some decent folk, and some not so decent folk — yes I was abused by some, then thrown out the vehicle. I was sixteen years old at that time, with not an ounce of sweetness left. I grew hard and bitter and remained so for the next five years. One kind woman, telephoned Catena to tell her where I was. The rest is history, the police picked me up and took me home. My parents did not want to know about it all, they threw me out, disowned me. They did not want to have my disgrace bringing disrepute to their business and family name — what family, I ask you? I took Catena with me to Florida, I nursed her at home through her later years, to the end of her days. I know I mistreated her in my headstrong days, but she was the only mother I knew.' Audra paused, a few stifled sobs could be heard in the room. Audra continued.

'My name was Sophia, I became Audra because that is what Ramón called me during our year together, he said I reminded him of Audrey Hepburn, in the movies Romina watched, but he liked to call me Audra. I run the *Audra House Foundation* in Florida for abused teenage girls. Very recently the government granted a subsidy to fund two more centres as the *Audra House Foundation*. Its reach is saving many neglected girls from wealthy and needy families from losing a grip on life. This is my story, for what it's worth. Thank you.'

Seventy-five women stood up, wiping away tears, applauding Audra's bravery and commitment to serving others. The applause continued to ring through the meeting centre until Masuyo walked in and took the microphone.

'Thank you, Audra! I watched and listened in my office. I too teared and gasped as you did. You are all phenomenal women, sacrificing your lives for others, I applaud you today and forevermore. May Truth, Understanding and Compassion always guide your actions.' She bowed and left the room.

Patience addressed the audience.

'Thank you, Audra, we have all gained many life lessons from your experience. If you have any questions for Audra, I recommend we write them down and discuss them next week, once all testimonies are complete. This revelation is emotionally draining, while also being cathartic for our brave speakers. Zuri advised me that lunch is served in the courtyard today. Truth, Understanding and Compassion to you.'

She was pleased that the sessions were recorded, she intended watching them all, much was to be gained.

16

Q & A

The emotions were heavy after two days of personal confessions. The reflective mood was etched on distracted faces, caught in a web of reveries. What Masuyo hoped to achieve was gained, the eye was now turned inward, celebrating the good in one's life, questioning what needed to be changed. It was time to move on from self-absorption.

A Q & A session was held the next morning in the large auditorium. Some questions were dangling in the minds of those most affected by the personal testimonies. Masuyo knew from personal experience that closure brought the greatest understanding on life's challenges. She stated that the mission's values stressed that Truth is always the trigger, Understanding is a slow process which ignites lifetime Compassion. Then it becomes impossible to turn off the switch. The mission was committed to this philosophy that was achievable through psychological manipulation.

A breakfast of fresh papaya, watermelon, kiwi-fruit, bananas, mangoes and persimmons with creamy yoghurt, and a large tub of coconut yoghurt was on offer. The strong, deep-roasted aroma of freshly ground coffee permeated the air. Patience waltzed towards the coffee table while Ming relished the fruit.

'I don't know how you don't start your day with a cup of coffee, Ming.'

'You might have two cups of coffee in your day, I sip green tea almost all day, so it goes down to the drink of choice, the stronger the drink, the less number of cups drunk per day.'

'Ming, you really think things through. I just gravitate towards the coffee as an unthinking survival act!' Patience laughed and had Ming giggling quietly as she crunched on the sweet, juicy fruit.

Some in the breakfast room smiled at them, enjoying Patience's loud morning banter with Ming. The mood was still heavy, uneasy with each not knowing how to broach the other on the revelations that had moved them. Patience and Ming had bonded since their first encounter en route to Singapore, they debriefed last night on Akanya's and Audra's personal histories. They were baffled by the strength both women exuded. Ming confessed she found the sessions stressful. Patience revealed she was exposed to similar situations with women who were rescued through her Sisters Helping Sisters Organisation in Australia. The safe house was where all reservation crumbled, and emotions were gaping wounds.

NEWS BUZZED around in some quiet conversations that Alva was back in the sanatorium, her stress levels had triggered her asthma, her breathing had declined, making it difficult for her to speak. Thoughts of what her personal history was, occupied thoughts that morning. She was a fiercely private young woman, who was doing valuable work in the world to have been selected. Ming spoke to Patience about what could have been the reasoning behind choosing a vulnerable young woman for this mission.

'I think she is here as a case study to track where she will go, and what else she will achieve because of her personal trauma. I think she's one to watch and learn from.'

'Wow that is astute thinking, and you said, *I* think things through. There's a psychologist in you, Patience!'

'Aren't we all, as women?'

Masuyo walked into the room, all activities, eating and quiet chats stopped in her presence.

EVERYBODY WAS SEATED IN SILENCE. Xandria held the microphone. She was flanked by Masuyo, Zuri, and Alexis.

'Truth, Understanding and Compassion to you. As you know from the late night notes slipped under your doors, the mission decided that this Q & A was necessary for greater understanding. You are now well-versed on the mission's values that Compassion is born from Understanding. This session should elevate your sensitivity on how these values are entwined. Audra and Akanya have graciously accepted to answer your questions as best as they can. Be gentle. The floor is now open for questions by a show of hands, please.'

Patience heard the diplomat and politician in Xandria's voice, her disposition was humble, but she was not a woman who would allow anyone to get away with being unkind.

Audra walked up to the podium, head bowed. A calm aura surrounded her, unlike her former feisty demonstrations in the early days at the mission.

'Truth, Understanding and Compassion, one and all, I feel like a newborn baby, naked before you. Pardon the cliché, but the truth does set you free. I no longer feel I have to wear a mask around you and I am assured by your attendance today, that indeed, you accept me for who I am. Share your personal histories, even if it's with each other, you will feel freer than you already are, revelation is beneficial to the soul.'

The first person to raise a hand was Deidre, the young delegate from Tasmania.

'Audra, thank you for your testimony. If I may add the name Audra is just beautiful for you.'

The large auditorium, filled to capacity, broke out in applause. Each row rose in synchronicity, bowing in their validation of Audra. With regimented precision, the women sat down.

Patience was blown away by how quickly they had become mission members. Daily rituals, the TUC greeting, partially bowed heads when speaking to each other, and stepping back while still facing the audience, had become second nature. The stillness of almost a hundred and fifty women, eager to hear the question posed to Audra, electrified the room.

'You mentioned that Ramón, God rest his soul, was shot after a voice called out to him in recognition. Did you know or find out what led to that fatal day? Was he involved in something that you might not have known about?'

'Thank you for your question, Deidre.'

The mood grew sombre, as hearts pounded, wanting to hear another layer to Audra's truth.

'Yes, I found out later, after Ramón's death, that his father was a known underground crime operator — this was the reason why he was sent to school in Louisiana to avoid becoming a victim of his father's illegal organisation. He was aware, I believe, of the line of work his father engaged in. He did not discuss any of that in our time together. Does that answer your question as you expected?'

'Yes, thank you, it does, but had you been told, would you have ended the relationship or avoided going to Mexico?'

'I loved Ramón. Apart from my nanny, Catena, I knew no other closeness until Ramón. I believe this would have made me stay in the relationship with him regardless of whether I knew his family's history or not. It's like being a wounded animal, you gravitate to warmth and kindness, ignoring dangerous possibilities because you believe you cannot be more wounded than you already are. Does that make sense?' Audra looked up at the faces etched with heavy sadness.

'Thank you, Audra, for opening up to us.'

Masuyo raised her hand. This caused a rustling of uneasy feet.

'Audra, you are an amazing woman, this is why we chose you. I am keen to know more on the decision to change your name. Names are significant to me, they label us, but I believe they define us too. Was it a bid to relinquish who you were, to become who you are?'

'Thank you for asking that significant question. Names are and should continue to be unique to each one of us. I don't have much faith in names these days that label children as objects. Sophia was my maternal grandmother's name, I never met her in life and did not hear anything spoken of her, so I have no ideas on whose name I was carrying. Had I known my grandmother in the flesh, or through what was revealed about her, the decision to change my name would have been difficult. I live and breathe being Ramón's Audra — he brought meaning in my life. He made me feel I had a right to be alive, loved and acknowledged.'

Another hand shot up from Saadaa, the Saudi Arabian delegate, 'did you meet another love in your life, Audra? You were so young when you faced the brutal taking of Ramón's life.'

'No, no other love entered my life. There were offers, attention was thrown my way — my heart was frozen in Ramón's name. I could not bring myself to set my heart aflame again.'

Another deafening round of applause filled the auditorium that morning. Patience had the urge to probe into Audra's parents' lives, she wanted to know if they were still alive, did they ever make contact with her again, would she visit them if the opportunity presented itself?

She left that lid unopened, sensing it was buried so deep, and shut with a heavy weight on it.

Akanya walked to the podium, dressed in a white silk sari.

Patience was surprised not to see her in their customary morning tracksuit. It dawned on her that the mission knew much about them and perhaps cultural costumes were available for everybody. How would the mission clothe her in cultural attire? She was vehement about saying she was a South African-Australian. She smiled at the memory of Mama Varuna's strong stance when asked about her nationality, she would always say, 'A proud Australian mate!' This created confusion which she added to when asked where she was from, she would simply say, 'Sydney.' Varuna loved her years in Australia and said she wished she had moved over when the girls were younger.

Akanya was graceful and serene. A large dot decorated the centre of her forehead. She clasped her hands together, closed her eyes and whispered, 'Truth, Understanding and Compassion. I respectfully add in my language, 'shanti,' as in my peace offering to you. Thank you for listening to my testimony. I have had overwhelming compassion from many since my session yesterday. Please proceed with your questions. Nothing is off limits, feel free to deepen your understanding of life in my cultural shoes. I know the mission supports global connectedness, look at us here!'

Patience waited for the applause to stop before she raised her hand.

'Akanya, you look amazing in your sari. You are maternal in all you do and say, would you attribute this entirely to the events that transpired in your childhood?'

'Thank you, Patience, I will happily show you how to don a sari' she laughed. Your question gives me the highest accolade in my culture. Mother is the ultimate, mother that gave me life to continue my life's mission on earth, is akin to a supreme being.'

A long, loud, 'Aaahhh' followed by a loud applause that lasted five minutes was quietened down when Xandria lifted her hand and asked Akanya to continue.

'I was called upon to act as mother to my step-brother because of my mother's predicament, but also by default, I was the eldest child in the family. This awakened the profound need within me to nurture, protect and love those in need, especially children. Yet, I don't have any children of my own. Let me correct that, I do have my own children, just not biological children.'

There were many moist eyes in the room with this further autobiographical revelation.

'Don't be sad for me. I am blessed with many young girls who I work with in empowering their technological skills to break the shackles of domestic or marital dependence, to allow them to shape their own journey through life.'

On this note the South Korean delegate raised her hand, 'Akanya did you choose not to have children after what happened to your mother?'

'This is a 'yes' and 'no' answer, Ji Su. Firstly I was not fortunate enough to meet my Mr. Darcy. I had hoped he would appear right out of the pages of Jane Austen's *Pride and Prejudice* to sweep me off my feet. I only got as close as a coffee mug with his face.' Akanya had moist eyes spring afresh with mirth as she exaggerated the size of the mug with her usual swooping rounded arm gesture and bobbing head, laughing at what she had just said.

'Jokes aside, when those young men on horseback stampeded our home, I was brutalised by what I later learned were army officers or soldiers from a neighbouring army barracks. With no immediate medical attention, I developed sepsis which, thankfully, did not claim my life, as it was thought it would, but it left me infertile.'

Another deep, sad, 'NOOOOO' echoed through the auditorium.

'I am blessed to be a mother to thousands of young women today. They very fondly refer to me as 'Kanya-ma' — music to my ears.

The women rose again chanting, *Kanya-ma, Kanya-ma, Kanya-ma,* building up to a frenzied chant, and ending with 'we love you, *Kanya-ma!*'

Akanya bowed with closed palms in salutation to the audience first, then Masuyo and her entourage. Her radiant smile as she exited the room, stepping backwards, was a bright, warm blast of sunshine.

Masuyo took the microphone and stepped out into the audience, walking around as she spoke.

'Mother and compassion are inseparable. We are wired before we are born to serve those in need, which include our men, some of whom serve maternal roles too. We must always remember, without us, there is no life, no joy, no care — you are immeasurably special, wonderful and needed. We chose you to make the world a better place for our sisters and brothers. I salute every one of you for embracing the mission's values and hopes. You questioned to gain Understanding asking for the Truth and here now we have further evidence of your Compassion. Peace be with you.'

She stepped backwards towards the exit leaving a calmness in the room.

17

DEGUSTATION

A bond developed between the recruits at Masuyo's mission. Her careful planning and thoughtful selection of the candidates meant she had the best in the world, the most giving to lead the next generation of women in their elected leadership roles. Now was a right time to engage a few in a cooking of cultural dishes to extend inclusiveness and create deeper connections. Through appreciation and understanding, the mission upheld that many roads lead to the same path of salvation, the one where peace is the ultimate.

Ming, Akanya, and Saadaa volunteered to prepare, Chinese, Indian and Middle Eastern dishes. They would also explain the cultural partaking of food within their cultures and respective families. It was to be an[1] educative gustatory experience. The catering team, who they had not met before was eager to assist them, and equally happy to let them have control of the state-of-the-art kitchen. Marble floors, high ceilings, copper, stainless steel and glass utensils were abundant, gleaming from behind glass-door cupboards. Ming was delighted with the chopping utensils, ideal for the enormous stir-fry and filling for the spring rolls she would prepare. A large, deep soup urn was perfect for her plum dipping sauce.

Akanya slipped into a vernacular explosion when she saw chillies, coriander and an array of Indian spices in quaint jars. She held up the coriander and inhaled the joy of home.

'I feel I'm home now!' Akanya laughed.

Ming smiled, understanding how the scent of coriander conjured wonderful memories.

'Our homes might not be all that different after all, coriander is my joy too!'

Saadaa added, 'be careful now, Akanya, don't get too comfortable here, you might not want to leave.'

'Well this could be my perpetual holiday on board this luxury liner, but only God knows from where to where.' Her large circular gesture emphasised the ignorance of their specific location.

'Destination and location unknown!' she laughed, her dancing doll head bobbed with glee. She then proceeded to chop up the onions in a teary haze.

'Use the food processor, Akanya, it has awesome chopping blades.' Ming said.

'Ah, no, too *fancy shmancy* for me! Good old fashioned hands work well for me!'

Saadaa had a steaming pot of chickpeas on the gigantic cooker and spoke with intimacy of her life.

'*Fancy shmancy* indeed, but quite frankly, I would rather be in my mother's kitchen. I miss her arms and chastisements now. She would correct my every move in the kitchen, I hated that, but right now, I will give anything to be hearing it. She must be ill with worry about my whereabouts.'

'We understand,' Ming said, 'but what makes it bearable is that we are treated with respect, all the mission ladies are gracious and caring.'

'I know, but it's not home as I know it. I wish you both would one day visit my family home in Lebanon. I promise, you won't want to leave.' Saadaa's wistful disposition conveyed how homesick she was. She came from a close-knit family, the youngest of six children. This was the first time she spoke as much, comfortable in this grand kitchen with women who were maternal in their respect for each other.

'Well, we are going to miss the 'live' Skype communication today with the outside world,' Akanya lamented, 'some of the ladies have been starved of a male face, hormones for some will be flying around, especially for Patience.'

Ming was quick to jump to Patience's defence.

'Look, Patience loves a good laugh and can be quite a tease at times. I don't believe she is 'starved' of male company in any way.' Ming looked at Saadaa, for her reaction, she was in her own world, lost in her thoughts of her mother and the warmth of home. She was as young as Zuri, no more than in her early twenties.

Ming was loyal to those who supported her. She was not going to let a jovial misrepresentation of her friend go without correcting it. Akanya was taken aback in seeing the fire in Ming's reaction - something she had not noticed before. She avoided a retort, electing silence on the subject.

ON THE OTHER side of the mission building, excitement was brewing as everyone rushed to their seats in the auditorium, ready for news from the outside.

The ceiling to floor screen lit up and crackled off, much to the dismay of the audience. Then another flicker and the face of a handsome man faded in and out.

A mournful, 'oh no!' passed through the room. Xandria took the microphone while Zuri worked on the screen panel.

'Ladies, please bear with us, technology at the best of times can let us down. I have a back-up plan, but let's give this another go. Zuri's expertise should get Judd Knight's face up soon!'

Patience nudged the person next to her, 'if we didn't know any better this could be straight out of George Orwell's *Nineteen Eighty-Four,* our *Orwellian* experience. What a story that would make when we got home!'

A rugged, square-jawed face, with quizzical eyes came up on the screen. Judd Knight was a tanned, glowing picture of health — bright, 'melt your heart' blue eyes peered as if trying to get a glimpse of his audience on the other side of the camera lens.

'Good day ladies, are you there? Holler back, 'yay!' so I know you can hear me until your image comes into focus.'

An almighty, 'yay!' rose up with the boom of a hundred voices.

'Ah, there you are! Lovely to hear you and see you now! How are you all?' Judd's caramel-rich, deep voice echoed in the room.

A school chorus of 'we are well, thanks Judd!' returned across the room.

'Glad to hear that. I am here to remind you that the work you are doing is spectacular, the sacrifice you're making does not go unnoticed.'

A 'thank you' shout out was returned to Judd.

'Firstly, I have news from around the world, which you have been patiently waiting for.' He paused, scanning the faces in the front row and continued.

'US politics seem to go on, as usual, nothing much has changed since your departure. US-Russian rumblings continue and on the Korean front, it appears that North and South are leaning towards affability — one to watch I daresay. South Africa has a new president, so that might mean the end of political corruption in that land. On the Australian front, the Catholic Church is still under scrutiny for child-sex crimes, and a trial is underway as we speak. Yet another one to watch closely. China continues to loom large in its economic growth. Sadly the crime against women has escalated, so we need you out soon to keep our sisters safe!'

On that last note, the house rose, applauding the call for the needed safety of women, articulated by a man. Judd Knight was a superhero in that moment.

He continued on the latest discoveries in science, medicine, the economy, and the rise of the Blockchain hype. He then introduced Dr Lara Williams who addressed women's health at length, taking into account the age range of the audience.

A Q & A followed after which Judd ran through a few relaxation exercises on how to 'protect your spine for an upright tomorrow.' His final comment had a few women dancing in the aisles, 'I will be out at the mission in two weeks, Masuyo will keep you posted. Have a good day ladies, keep happy, keep healthy, and keep dancing!' He flicked off the screen to the sound of a few more, 'ahhh's.'

Patience moved across the room to chat to Deidre, 'now, that was refreshing, getting a bit of news on what's going on outside. Not too much has changed which is gratifying, although not all of it is good.'

'I agree,' Deidre added, 'I appreciate that we had this update. At least we know our families, god willing, are safe.'

'Now, there's a thought, a Skype call to family, one can only dream,' Patience sighed.

Audra joined the Australasian duo at the refreshment table.

'It will be good to have different company with Judd's visit to the mission, I wonder when we will be told about his actual arrival day. I have no idea how people get here other than a flight in like we did.'

'I've stopped thinking about that now, I figured what's the point fretting over what I can't control, and that I'm safe is all that matters, right?' Patience responded.

Morgan Smith from North Queensland walked up to Deidre and Patience and introduced herself.

'Finally, we meet, Morgan,' Patience said with a broad smile, 'I'm surprised it took so long to realise there was another delegate from Australia, and we had no idea either of us existed in Australia, yet we are in a similar line of work.'

'Better late in the land of nowhere, instead of never,' Morgan laughed. 'Australia is a vast country after all. I rarely get out of Queensland. The children at the orphanage keep me busy. You must visit us sometime. I'd love to have you and Deidre over.'

'That would be an awesome experience,' Patience declared, 'who knows we might be able to work together on some social justice initiatives.'

'Do you both have families at home? Have you written to them yet?' Morgan asked.

'Yes, my sister should be receiving my letter any day now, how about you?'

'I sent a letter to the children I care for. They are my family. It is home to me. I was raised there.' Morgan smiled, avoiding eye contact.

Deidre and Patience were choked, but admired the profound calm acceptance of her life and community involvement.

THE CULTURAL DEGUSTATION that night filled the longing for what each called home. Akanya proved to be a wonderful hostess, ensuring everyone had a taste of what she prepared with a brief history of the ingredients and cooking process. She had a bevy of women writing down the recipe to her gustatory creation. Patience relished the chilli, floating into seventh heaven with each explosive, spicy bite. Those who could not have too much spice, tucked into the spring rolls, plum dipping sauce and falafels accompanied by a rich hummus dip. Saadaa smiled, knowing her mother would be so proud of her culinary skills and hospitality, a hallmark of her culture and family togetherness.

A stronger bond was forged that night as many countries united as family sharing a meal.

18

FRAGILITY

Grace went about her daily life with a heaviness, forcing herself to be in the moment with Keefe and ahead of her game on the job front. Andrew Lang continued to be her source of motivation and support.

Fear grew with no new information surfacing on the missing plane and passengers — Grace's mounting fear was that like other cold cases, Patience might become another statistic in the history of missing aircrafts, her life would be in eternal limbo. She religiously checked all social media sites in the hope there might be breaking news, and she made weekly calls to the Australian delegates' families. They found friendship in their fear and dread of loss. Grace pondered on the mystery of life, its beauty and terror that challenges invited. Her life was suspended with fear and need, she did not have her sister to confide in.

Marriage was not her priority, not now anyhow, but she was all too aware of Keefe's need to bring joy to his mother's world.

SHE ARRIVED at ER that evening, determined to conquer the sinking feeling that pervaded her world.

Andrew was his usual cheerful self.

'Hi, Grace, I have a pot of coffee ready, the finest I could find this weekend at a coffee expo at Olympic Park. May I pour you a cup?'

Grace knew that Andrew avoided asking her how she was, or if she had more news.

'Thank you, Andrew, I would love a cup. There's a nip in the air tonight, winter is creeping in.'

'It sure is. I picked up my overcoat from the dry cleaners this weekend. I'm bracing myself for colder nights. The walk from the car park chills me, and it takes a while to thaw in here.'

'Yeah, that tunnel of cold, blustery air as you get closer to the building is what I find very chilly indeed. Thanks, this coffee is just what I needed. Where can I get a pack of this aromatic beans?'

'I have a pack for you, it's on your desk. We have to prepare ourselves, ahead of time this year, for an increase in burn victims. Last year was catastrophic!'

'Thank you for the coffee beans, you are always so thoughtful. Yeah, last year there were far too many hot-water bottle and heater accidents that could have been avoided. I don't know how we're going to prevent this when the elderly are vulnerable at this time of year.'

'We need more awareness campaigns, or home visits if the government is prepared to fund it. Let's hope it's not too bad this year. How's Keefe doing?' Any more news on his mum's condition?'

'He's well, thanks. His mother's health is declining a lot faster now, he's keen to go over to Ireland as soon as possible.' She trailed off, unsure of what else to say.

'How about you? Have you given it careful thought? I mean about going with him?'

Grace was lost in thought for a brief moment, but surprised Andrew when she said, 'I'm considering it. I have to commit to meeting his family at least. He says he is a keeper although he monkeys around saying *keefer,* and that there's no hope that he's ever going away!' She smiled in awkward acknowledgement of her intimate revelation. Andrew knew her well, she too was not going anywhere in life without her newfound *keefer.* She was different when she returned from her dreaded conference in Amsterdam. There was a spark that Andrew enjoyed seeing. He knew that someone had touched her heart. He had to be happy for her, it meant a lot to him to see her this way. His heart had never stopped yearning.

'He's a good man, hang onto him. We have to move with life's challenges, not against it, if we ever hope to recover in strength.'

Grace absorbed Andrew's words before she said, 'I will remember that, thanks.'

She walked back to her office to prepare for a staff briefing.

AT TEN FORTY-FIVE THAT NIGHT, a six-month-old baby girl was brought in with breathing difficulties. She was being treated by a family paediatrician for a cough and cold. The baby had a tinge of blue around her forehead and mouth. The red-eyed mother was in her mid-forties, a school teacher, and the father, a freelance IT consultant in his mid-fifties — he presented as anxious and unable to stop the flood of tears running down his face. Paramedics administered oxygen, but the baby was unresponsive.

Grace kicked into action like a button was pressed. Every nerve and pulse was ready to get a sign from the still, tiny little girl. She punched out questions to the parents as Nurse Beth Hobbs swaddled the baby in a thermal blanket. Her little body was cold. The blueness around the mouth was spreading to her neck.

'What time did you last feed her?'

'When did she commence taking the medication she is on?'

'How long did you take after she was unresponsive before you called for medical assistance?'

The baby's father was mute, consumed by his emotions and frazzled by the questions Grace asked. The mother answered in a calm, composed voice. She looked at her little girl and then at Grace with searching confusion.

'Will she pull through, doctor? She had a cold, that is all she had, now…'

Grace felt the lump in her throat harden, she had to ignore it.

'We will do all we can to ease her breathing, her vital signs are not promising at this stage, but we will try our level best.'

'Thank you Dr Sharvin. Is there anything my husband and I can do to help?'

'Be here, hold her hand and talk to her. Her body is weak but she may respond to your voice and touch.'

Grace knew the flu virus was debilitating, it had come to be known as the 'Sydney Flu' around the world. If the baby was exposed to that particular strain of the flu, Grace feared the outcome for her delicate little body. She had a battle on her hands.

Training for many months under Dr Grace Sharvin had improved Nurse Beth Hobbs medical skills, her bedside manner was compassionate. She was able to assess the severity of the impact of trauma on the patient, and was demonstrating that her job was important to her. Her emotions ran as deep as Grace's when a patient did not make it back home.

The baby's heartbeat grew stronger although she was still in danger. As much as Grace wanted to promise that all will be well, it was too early to make that assessment.

Beth Hobbs approached Grace with grave concern.

'Dr Sharvin, what do you think? Will the little cherub's body withstand the medication, is her heart strong enough for this?'

'Beth, I'm living in hope. Seeing the parents hanging on with every breath they have, as they look to me for consolation, is unnerving. To state it plainly, the prognosis is not good at all.'

A quiet, red-faced Beth walked out of Grace's office for a private sob in the ladies' room.

AT FIVE MINUTES PAST TWELVE, the little girl drew her last breath. The gut-wrenching sob from the mother, followed by the sight of both parents clinging to each other in the loss of their only child — a gift that came to them as a surprise after many years of marriage. Now that joy was gone.

Grace knew that more had to be researched on the dreaded virus that had claimed a few lives. She struggled to accept that medical science had come this far, and yet had no answers for how to overcome its debilitating impact. Death of a patient in ER left Grace fragile for a few days. She played out all the possible scenarios over and over again. Could she have done something better?

Keefe was a pragmatist on life and death. His emotional side was separated from his professional side which Grace could not quite understand.

'You did everything in your medical capacity to save the patient, you eased any pain she might have had. It's a virus that has not been isolated and understood. You cannot mourn the loss of your patients to the detriment of your own wellbeing. You must learn to cope with this, it's the only way we can survive in this profession to serve others better. Grace you are a gift to the profession, but don't let it consume you.'

She needed to hear his words, her head and heart were her worst enemies.

Keefe took out the garbage for her that night, and brought in the mail while she heated up dinner for them. They ate in silence with the television news playing softly in the background. Grace cleared up, picked up the mail off the hallway desk — a letter with a Singapore postmark caught her attention. She ripped it open. Patience's handwriting smiled up at her. She read it through twice, ignoring Keefe's question on who the letter was from.

She passed it to Keefe, unsure if she wanted to hear his opinion.

'Thank God, she's alive Grace!'

'I know. I'm grateful for that. It seems she is in Singapore as per the postmark. They were thrown off course within an hour after take-off. She is in an undisclosed location and the people are good, she says. Why is she in the dark about her location?'

'Let's hang onto the fact she is alive, and as she says, she seems to be safe and will return home at some point.'

'I am grateful for that Keefe, don't get me wrong. Is she being held against her will and is afraid to say so? I don't have a reply address which confirms to me she being held hostage, and might have written the letter under duress.'

'Don't get worked up on this. Sleep on it tonight and report to the investigating team tomorrow. It's significant enough for them to know you received a letter from Singapore. Patience also indi-cates she will write again.'

'Yeah, I suppose that is all I can do.'

'I'm staying over tonight in Patience's room to give you space if that's acceptable by you Dr Sharvin?' Keefe smiled, putting his arms around her.

Grace felt a surge of warmth course through her body as she acknowledged how lucky she was to have Keefe in her life.

'No, Dr Daly, while you are under my roof, you will sleep in my bed. I need your arms of comfort tonight.'

Keefe smiled the same quiet smile she saw for the first time, at the conference in Amsterdam, when Nina Holstead introduced her to the foreign delegates.

She tugged his arm and led him to her room.

19

MAM AND AILEEN

Grace walked with a somewhat lighter step. The knowledge that her sister was alive, sustained her, bringing light back into her world. The pendulum of life swings both ways, hope on one hand, and fear that the end is nigh. Grace agreed to join Keefe on a week-long trip to Ireland to see his ailing mother. Their busy work cycle did not permit taking more time out.

With Andrew heading ER as her assistant, Grace had more flexibility to attend to her personal needs. His aching heart knew that this journey would seal Grace's relationship with Keefe. He had to move on, to stop living in hope. Regardless of what fate awaited either of them, he knew their friendship was a life-long one.

THE SUMMER HAD JUST BEGUN in Ireland, everything looked fresh, quite green after the April showers. They arrived at Belfast City Airport on a cool morning. Grace reached for her light cardigan, glad she could shrug off her overcoat. First stop was to offload their luggage at Keefe's apartment before they headed to Royal Victoria Hospital to see his mother.

'Now, don't mind the state of my place, it might be dusty after being locked for so many months. We could go to a hotel if it's not suitable.'

'Don't be silly, a quick clean is all it might need — I am reasonably good with household chores, in case you didn't notice,' Grace smiled, 'we will be out most of the time anyway.'

'Aye, you're probably right. My sister will meet us at the hospital after work tonight. I suggested we go out for dinner to get you two better acquainted. What do you think?'

'Sounds like a plan, I'm happy with whatever you wish, it's your week so give me at least an hour's notice, and all should be fine.'

Keefe cast a loving, puppy-eyed look across Grace's face as they jumped into the taxi. He knew this trip is what she needed too, to offer her a semblance of reprieve from her concerns over Patience. He was desperate for his mother to meet her, the woman who had finally arrived in his life after a few failed relationships, his marriage of five years ago being the worst by far. The scars from that last mistake kept him single and enmeshed in his work life until he met the gentle, quiet, vulnerable Grace Sharvin in Amsterdam.

'I warn you, you might regret giving me the reins in my territory!' His eyes sparkled at this thought. 'I want you to have a glimpse of my home country too.'

Grace was happy to go along with his plans, she welcomed any distraction while she waited for another letter from Patience.

'I will have to avoid some of my work colleagues this week, it's a short trip and meeting them will mean it becomes a beer fest day! I don't intend leaving you alone if I can help it.'

'I don't mind, if you want to have an evening with the boys, go ahead, I have some paperwork to catch up on. I won't be at a loose end if that's what you're concerned about.'

'Workaholic! No, I don't intend to be out with the boys for a *craic!*'

Grace loved Keefe's relaxed *Irishness*. He was comfortable in his skin around her.

'I will have a *craic* on my own, don't you worry about that!'

'When I finish with you, you will sound like you were born here. Well, there's my street, my apartment is the one in the corner there.'

Keefe's apartment was immaculate. Fresh roses adorned the coffee table, beside it was a gigantic card emblazoned with the words, 'Welcome Home Grace!'

Grace stood at the doorway to the lounge room for a few seconds.

'So much for a dusty apartment, Keefe!'

I organised a cleaner through my sister, and she must have added the flowers and card. She is a very thoughtful person.'

'Thank you, that is a lovely, kind gesture. I can't wait to meet your mother and Aileen.'

They found the fridge filled with milk, eggs, cheese, and a loaf of bread was left on the kitchen counter. Aileen's gesture reminded Grace of what Patience or she would do, when either one was returning from a trip.

THEY ARRIVED at the hospital around three o' clock that afternoon. Mrs Daly was in high care. Grace sensed Keefe's anxiety as they walked towards his mother's ward. His hands were locked in his pockets, he stared at the ground, walking with a fast-paced deliberate step.

The senior nurse on duty recognised Keefe, she walked up to

him. Grace stood a few paces behind him. She shook his hand, and Grace heard the gist of their lowered conversation.

'She's had some good days and not so good days. This past weekend she took a bit of a knock on new meds, but they were necessary. She tires easily so give her some rest breaks while you are in there with her. Don't overexcite her.'

Keefe motioned to Grace to come closer.

'Cara, this is my fiancé, Grace Sharvin, a medic in Australia.'

Grace stepped forward blushing, her ears were hot from hearing herself being referred to as Keefe's fiancé for the first time.

'Oh, lovely to meet you, Grace,' Cara cooed. Her warm spirit was hard to miss.

She led them to the private ward and went in before them to announce Keefe's arrival. He didn't want to overly excite his mother by appearing unannounced at her bedside.

Grace stood behind Keefe, out of sight, to allow him a moment on his own with his mother. She heard his mother say, 'Where's Grace, Aileen told me she was coming with you?'

'She's here mam and very keen to meet you. Come in Grace and meet my mam, Colleen Daly. Mam this is Grace, my love. So, what do you think?' He laughed, looking at Grace for acknowledgement.

Grace cowered, her shoulders drooped as she waited to be greeted.

'So lovely to meet you, Grace. What a beautiful name your mam gave you, to match your lovely face. Here, hold my hand, I would plant a kiss on that face if I could,' she smiled.

The welcome she received, melted her customary reserve when meeting people for the first time, least of all, Keefe's mam.

'Thank you, so lovely to finally meet you, mam.' She knew her mother would expect no other way of addressing Keefe's mother.

His face reddened with emotion as Grace held mam's hands, and bent over to kiss her on the forehead. He stood close to Grace with his left hand on her shoulder and his right hand stroking the top of mam's head.

'So happy you are here with Grace, my boy. Aileen will be in later, after work.'

'Rest mam, I will do all the talking about what I've been getting up to in Australia.'

Her blue eyes gleamed as she looked at Grace and then Keefe. Grace saw those very eyes when she first met Keefe in Amsterdam.

She absorbed this precious, shared family time, remembering the time before her father's death and the many nights spent in conversation, sharing stories.

Family was a necessary connection, to feel safe, valued and loved.

KEEFE EXCUSED himself to meet with mam's physician for an in-depth understanding of where she was in the treatment process. As much as it was a sore point with him, he had to put his medic hat on to deal with the time frame mam had left. He coped with patients' deaths as an unavoidable expectation, in extreme cases, in his care of them. He was shattered to hear that mam had six weeks to three months at the very most.

Grace received a short text message saying he will be back in an hour. No explanations were given. She knew that this was his week, but, she expected to be kept in the loop of where he was, and what he was doing.

Mam was reassured by Grace that Keefe would be back soon. She motioned to the draw next to her bed and told Grace to look through the photo album.

'It will give you an idea of Keefe's family, more on his father and extended family. Grace flicked through, keeping her questions to a minimum to avoid tiring mam.

She knew Keefe's father died during a bomb blast in Belfast forty years ago. Keefe was just five years old and Aileen was eight at the time. Mam raised the children single-handedly, working nights at the dry cleaning business and cleaning the homes of the wealthy by day. She was determined that her children would get a good education and break the cycle of poverty she endured after her husband's death. Her dream was realised when Aileen was sworn in as a barrister, and six years later again when Keefe took up a position as a medical doctor in Belfast.

Grace felt the rough, dry skin on mam's palms when she held her hands. Her fingers were twisted and knobbly from an early onset of arthritis.

'It was hard, Grace, but look, my pride and joy.' She looked towards the door as though Keefe and Aileen were there. 'Tell me a bit about your mam.'

In her time of grave illness, mam had the sensitivity to want to know about her mother. Grace was careful not to let on about Patience's situation, in the fear it might unsettle her. She had a pact with Keefe, not to talk about Patience's disappearance. Grace was Grace, fiercely private about her emotional being and her personal world.

She felt a tinge of guilt when mam said, 'only child, it must have been lonely.' Mam sympathised that both she and Keefe had lost their fathers at a young age.

KEEFE ARRIVED TWO HOURS LATER. Grace smelt beer on his breath. This was the first time she saw him this way, hair dishevelled, out of sorts and distant. He couldn't make eye contact with her. In a moment of anger, she thought, how dare he do this when his mother is ill. I'm here with him and he goes off to a pub for more than one drink? He knows we have limited time in Belfast, how insensitive of him! Is this the beginning of something I'm being made aware of?

Nothing was said about where he was or what mam's physician had said to him.

At five-thirty that afternoon Aileen arrived. She took one look at Keefe and prodded him on the arm with her index finger.

'Been drinking before dinner, that's odd, you have no shame that your lady is here for the first time, do you?' Her stern look was enough to make Grace uncomfortable.

'Look, Aileen, later, it's a long story. We have half an hour here and have to leave. The head nurse says it has been a long, excitable day for mam. We can head off for some dinner.'

Mam was in her element with all three around her bedside. There was a hint of colour in her cheeks when they kissed her and parted.

After a grilled fish and salad dinner, Grace and Keefe headed back to his apartment. Aileen whispered loud enough for Grace to catch what she planted in Keefe's ear before she left— 'text me and let me know.'

'What was that about?'

'Nothing much, just checking if we need anything else in the apartment.'

Back at the apartment, Keefe broke the awkward silence between them.

'I'm so sorry Grace for disappearing, I could not face mam after the doctor said...'

'Is it about the time she has left?'

'Aye, six weeks to three months, Grace, that is all she has.'

'I'm so sorry Keefe. She reached out to hold his hand. 'I thought it would be a year at the very least, I'm so sorry. I can return to Australia, you should stay on.'

'No, I can't.'

'Why not?'

'I have to get back to tie up a few things to come back for an extended stay. I did not expect this. Aileen did not give me any details. I don't think she has any idea. I did not mean to desert you this afternoon.'

'No time to be sorry now, we must think and act with speed. I thought it was out of character for you to disappear, and I was shocked to see you in that state.' She moved closer to him, hooking her arm through his.

'Thank you for being here and understanding. Poor mam, she worked so hard to give us a good life, you know.'

'She told me a bit about her life after your father died, and I saw a photograph of you when you were just a babe, toothless, freckled and adorable!'

'You don't think I'm adorable now? I suppose not with my stinking beer breath.'

Grace laughed allowing Keefe to relax.

'Don't say anything until I've finished saying what I have to say. I've asked you to marry me and you have not given me an answer yet. Can you answer me now?'

He went down on one knee, held both her hands, 'Grace Sharvin, will you marry me, please Grace.'

She looked at him, killing him with her silence at first, 'I will Keefe, I will, but I can't promise when I'll be ready to tie the final knot, what with Patience...?'

'Thank you, I'm over the moon that you said 'yes' I can wait to tie the knot for as long as it takes.' He pulled out the black and gold box from inside his jacket for the second time, after his last failed attempt. He slipped the ring on Grace's finger and clung to her like his life depended on the moment. 'Tomorrow is mam's birthday, I want to take this news to her, she will be so happy to know we are taking the next step in our commitment to each other. Mam can rest knowing this. I can tell she is quite taken with you.'

'I don't have a dress, just slacks on this trip Keefe... how... where?'

'Don't worry too much, we can do this proposal again in

Sydney. I know Andrew will want to be in on the celebrations too. Oh, what a time, my joy and sadness at the same time. I wish I had met you years ago... but am thankful for now...'

'What about Aileen, shouldn't you be telling her too?'

'She knows, that's why she told me to send her a text message. If you said, 'yes', she would meet us with a birthday come engagement cake at the hospital tomorrow.'

'You both are incorrigible, colluding behind my back!' Grace was shocked at the speed with which things were moving — she understood that mam was on limited time.

'So, is this a 'yes, I am happy to be engaged in my slacks' then?' Keefe laughed.

'Yes, Dr Daly it seems it is.'

He lifted her up in his arms, whispering into her hair, 'You've made me the happiest man alive, Dr Sharvin.'

KEEFE AND GRACE went to the hospital the next day. The engagement ring was carefully back in the box to re-enact the marriage proposal for mam. Aileen had the moment planned with hospital staff joining in on the double celebration — celebrating the life and love of mam and Keefe's and Grace's love and new life together. Mam politely asked if the solemnisation of the marriage would take place in Belfast because she would not be able to travel to Australia, what with her ailing health and all. Grace was silent, heavy with emotion that mam had no idea that her life's clock was on its final revolution. Before Keefe could say anything, Grace agreed that their marriage would be in Ireland. Keefe knew in the eyes of the Catholic Church he would not be allowed a church wedding, because he was divorced. After a few photographs were taken around mam's bed, they headed off for a quiet drink, and walk around the city. Aileen spent the afternoon with mam, sharing in the joy of Keefe's and Grace's happiness.

Keefe took Grace on his personalised tour of the political murals around the city — they held a special sad place in his heart, given the circumstances under which his father died. They walked hand in hand, lost in the union of their recent commitment to each other. Two days later they left for Sydney with Keefe's return flight booked a week later.

20

VISITORS

Judd Knight and an entourage of beauticians, hair and nail artists were on site at the mission. How and when they arrived was a mystery.

Judd ran three sessions on the days he was there. He ran smaller groups of a maximum of twenty women. He was dressed in mission attire, a pale grey track suit with TUC embroidered down the sleeves and outer sides of the pants. The beauty crew was hard to miss in their leather jackets and pants, pink and green hair, and bright red lipstick, making it difficult for them to blend in with the serene aura around them.

The mood had lifted, there was a bustling air in the need to enhance hair, nails, and skin. Feminine wiles needed attention after almost two months without pampering. The timetable for the three days was announced, and everybody wanted a piece of the pamper pie!

Patience booked in her hair braiding and beading session, surprised that it was possible. Ming had her hair cut very short, a close-cropped look, making her appear like a teenage boy.

'I can't have my hair hanging about my shoulders, I find it a hindrance to what I need to do, and hair that length needs too much care. I need to feel the breeze on my neck,' she laughed explaining her minimalist look.

'Whatever brings you joy girl, you go for it. These braids help me hang onto my culture. They make me feel like an African Queen!' Patience twirled around in a mock curtsy to Ming. They felt like school girls again, enjoying the presence of the visitors at the mission.

Akanya had an up-style hairdo making her look regal and ready for an Indian wedding. Audra dyed her hair red, refreshing her exhausted look.

All attempts to engage in conversation outside their roles was ignored by the stylists. Whispers surfaced among a few that they might be under strict instruction to only do what they were there for.

Judd's yoga and meditation sessions were welcome, bringing both mirth and a calm energy. He focused on the resonance of the 'om' sound, starting off at an elevated pitch and moving as low as his voice would go. He made it clear from his introductory session that there was no religion attached. His aura was much like that of Masuyo's, except that he was larger in spirit and joy. His booming voice and laughter were pronounced in a place where a male voice was absent. He bowed with every TUC greeting, the words rolled off his tongue with reverence. He had the mesmerising ability to address everyone like no one else was in the room.

'Patience, your braids do become you, Audra your passion shines through with that colour. Namaste Akanya, you are glowing.'

He stole into all their hearts during his brief days there.

He, too, was cautious in answering questions on where he hailed from. All he offered was, 'I am from the mission head office. You are halfway through your training and have big decisions to make about continuing to serve as a delegate of the mission, for another three months. It's not mandatory, as Masuyo would have explained.

He mingled among the ladies during breakfast and lunch but did not turn up to the dinners. The stylists had their own dining area — Patience saw this as a ploy to avoid socialising and getting too comfortable, lest their tongues took control. On the morning of the third day, the stylists disappeared without a formal goodbye.

NEWS BUZZED around that Alva's health was in danger. Masuyo called an emergency meeting to abort their speculations.

'Truth, Understanding and Compassion to you all. Our dear sister, Alva is unwell as you know. We have decided to send her back home, although she is keen to complete her training here. We advise that for her safety, she should return to her family and medical doctor.'

Audra's hand shot up before Masuyo could complete what she had to say. Questions bubbled in her head, she wanted concrete answers.

'Surely, with due respect, Masuyo, Alva cannot travel alone back to Sweden? How will this be arranged? How will she travel?'

'Thank you for your compassionate concern, Audra, Judd Knight will ensure her safe return to her home country.'

'How will they get to Sweden from here?'

'Transportation is arranged, she will depart from here as soon as our medic gives the clearance to do so.'

Audra wriggled in her seat, uncomfortable with the vague responses she received. Nobody seemed uneasy by her questions or Masuyo's answers. She leaned in towards Akanya who was sitting next to her.

'Not a very revealing answer, is it? Not even a direct answer to my question.'

Akanya shot her a cold stare, and hissed under her breath, 'leave it, Audra!'

'Why should I leave it, what if it was you and not Alva in this situation? We have a right to know exactly how she will leave and when.'

'She will be safe and that is all that matters, don't interfere.'

'Interfere? Your passive attitude is odd, you're a woman who speaks her mind, telling everybody off with your 'motherly' advice and yet you... you...'

Masuyo made it known she was observing Audra's agitation.

'Audra, if you have any concerns, please address them directly to me. I suggest you book a private session with me as soon as possible.'

Her usual humble tone had a sharp edge. Akanya nudged Audra in irritation.

'Look at what you've done. Please stop.'

'I'll talk to you later Akanya.'

Xandria and Alexis handed out questionnaires for the movie, *Erin Brockovitch* which was set as a case study that afternoon, with a before dinner discussion session.

Patience flicked through the questions. On the first page, the bold type caught her attention. It read: *How will you apply the skills gained from viewing the film to your new placement communities where you will serve and train young women?'* The use of 'will' twice in one bold statement was enough to suggest a command and finality which unnerved her.

Akanya and Audra stood talking outside the dinner room. Audra was red-faced, her neck taut, her expression set in anger.

Akanya stood with a straight, rod-iron back, her expression gave nothing away, except one who was listening carefully.

'I know we are safe and comfortable here, it's an artificial world. We need more information on how Alva will leave here. It's not enough to be told that Judd Knight will accompany her. We need specifics.'

Akanya thought through her response to avoid a further heated argument on the matter — Audra was off on an angry rant.

'For me, it's enough to know Alva is safe in being sent home. Lord knows, I would like to be sent home too, but not in illness. Fair enough we do not know how she will leave. My instinct tells me she will be air-lifted, the same way we came in to the mission.'

'I can't accept that, but will be quiet on the matter now.'

'Good to hear that, Audra. Try not to upset the apple-cart as it were, especially after that shift in Masuyo's attitude.'

'Awww, shucks, you can't be serious! She's a typical politician, never giving straight answers. Not asking questions will not make things easier. It spells that we are pliable.'

'We should go in for lunch. Patience is looking our way, which means we are inviting negative attention. Remain calm, more will come to light.'

AFTER VIEWING THE FILM, robust thoughts filled all conversations. The question Masuyo wanted answers for how they would implement the ideas in creating a new world order of future women leaders.

The ability to confront organisations that marginalised and exploited single mothers was a passionate point for Masuyo. She stepped onto the platform, and was bathed in strobe flashes of light that made her an alien presence.

'Persistence ladies is what you have to enforce in leading our young women into the future, speaking their truths must be prioritised and sustained. This must be vocal. If you fail, rise again until you get our young women believing in the power that they have.' Her face was hard in the light and shadow of the strobe lighting spinning around her. Her voice reverberated through the speaker. It hit the back wall and bounced back to her, adding intense volume to her usual soft voice.

Patience observed Masuyo with interest — this bold, digging-her-heels-in attitude suggested it was crunch time at the mission. No more 'soft' no more 'love all.' This was about being gutsy, and going after change to remove male world domination. Being gutsy was not an issue, the force Masuyo was intimating needed to be explained in specific terms. She continued, 'I want you to visualise yourself in a community of your choice, not your own community — how would you apply the Erin Brockovitch effect?'

The empowerment message was clear. Some women embrace this with immediacy. Their eyes were closed, lost in their mental communities. Others walked around the room talking, engaging on adversaries, and speaking out on injustice against women.

Xandria and Alexis stood up, chanting, urging the women to join in.

'Women unite! Women rise!'

They stood with right arms lifted, fists clenched in salute to the power of the slogan. Over and over again, the chanting continued as voices grew louder, harmonised in the euphoria of its meaning.

The revolution was sealed.

～

LATE THAT NIGHT Patience slipped out of her room, making her way to the conference room, in search of her misplaced reading glasses. As she passed the foyer, she stopped when she heard the

loud stuttering sounds of a helicopter, hovering somewhere overhead. She considered for a moment if it could be the generators
in the building that sounded louder when all were asleep.

She dashed into the foyer, the doors were shut.

She heard the fading sound of a helicopter as it sped off into
the distance.

21

MING'S HISTORY

Patience was restless, disturbed by the late-night sounds of the helicopter she knew she was not meant to hear. Confused thoughts emerged leaving her questioning whether it was Alva who was air-lifted out of the mission? Why the clandestine departure in the middle of the night? She felt a gnawing agitation that Grace might not have received her letter. Could it have been intercepted? Could Masuyo be trusted? Was the mission a cult organisation? Crazy thoughts whirred around in her head until the alarm went off for rise-up.

She had to gather herself to be there for Ming today, it was her revelation morning. After a hurried shower, she sped off to the dining hall, desperate to speak to Ming before her session.

'Truth, Understanding and Compassion, Patience,' she heard Ming's soft voice behind her, 'you look exhausted.'

Patience was uncomfortable, forcing herself to attentive — she could not possibly disturb Ming with her rambling suppositions. She knew the sound of the helicopter was close, above her, this meant they were below ground, what else could it be? She had to stop drifting into these abysmal thoughts.

'A little tired but nothing a cup of coffee can't cure. Don't worry about me, you have a big morning, how are you feeling?'

'I'll get you coffee, sit tight and relax. I'm a little nervous about my session, but if you keep your eye on me, I will be comforted.'

'Let's get coffee together. I'll be there eyeballing you the whole way through, you'll feel the burn, girlfriend!' Laughter was Patience's outlet to easing tension, it got her into a lot of trouble at school. Her report card comment often cited, 'Patience is advised to be serious about her learning.' She was not top of her year group, but she brought sunshine to every cloudy day.

'You know you can decline if you don't feel like going through with this.'

'It's something I have to do, and what better place than here where I know I'm accepted. I've never spoken publicly about my life. I've been too afraid to speak up.'

'It will be a cathartic experience, I know this from what the ladies in our safe houses go through. They feel a sense of sublime relief once they share their pain. You should take a walk on your own to gather your thoughts and emotions, your session is in forty-five minutes.'

Ming headed off for a walk. Patience watched her leave, nervous that Ming's calm disposition might be altered after the session. Each person's revelation, depending on the nature of the disclosure had different outcomes. She felt awful withholding this possible truth. Should she have cautioned Ming that she might be unsettled thereafter? She shrugged it off as Ming's decision, she would be there to support her.

Akanya followed Patience on her second trip to the coffee dispenser.

'Good morning, Patience, how are you? How is Ming, I saw her leave? Everything okay?'

'Truth, Understanding and Compassion to you this morning, Akanya.'

'Oops, sorry, I slipped up there, thinking I was back home, Truth, Understanding and Compassion to you too.'

'No apology necessary, I think we are a little homesick now. Ming took a walk to get ready for her session. She's a strong woman. I daresay fear can consume one at the thought of baring one's soul. I spent most of my childhood in fear that I did not deserve the privilege of two caring mothers.'

'I'm glad Ming is in control. I would love to know your story soon.'

Patience avoided a response.

'How are you feeling about our deployment locations being announced on Friday? Are you staying on for the extra months to serve the mission?'

Akanya's furrowed brow indicated her discomfort about the forthcoming announcement. Patience was unsure why Akanya hesitated. She shelved the uncomfortable thought of talking about her helicopter encounter. It could get misconstrued as her hallucination at that hour, or a bout of sleepwalking! Although Akanya had let them into her world, there was a part of her that did not quite make sense, just when she thought they were on the same wavelength about the mission, Akanya's reactions left her confused.

'Yes, I will serve the extra three months, but I'm keen to know if we can contact our families or colleagues while we are out doing field work.'

'That is a sore point with me, I must admit because there's no answer on that from Masuyo. I'm taking up the extra months too.'

Akanya admired Patience's level-headed approach to things, and her calm ability to invite anyone into her social space. She was comfortable and confident with who she was, this intrigued Akanya, sparking her curiosity to know more, to perhaps achieve the same in her life.

Patience was relieved to have some alone time with her private thoughts when Akanya walked away to start up a conversation with Audra. She missed Grace's sensitivity and stillness, pondering whether she had received her letter. She promised herself she would write to Felicity and Virginia Bale. Ajax's and Sprite's big slobbery licks were a comforting thought too. Home beckoned. She fluctuated between staying the course and yearning for home. It was difficult to toss the scepticism that crept back after last night. She was shaken from her reverie when she thought she heard a voice say, *stick with it Patience, don't give up.*

The voice of her spiritual mother, the loving Varuna, was reeling her in from wayward thoughts, just as she did in her childhood. She had to get a grip on her wandering thoughts before she began hallucinating, and sleepwalking! Being tossed into the sanatorium like Alva disturbed her equilibrium. She needed her sister's common sense more than ever.

Her strength returned in the knowledge that Sharvin women picked themselves up and moved on during a crisis. Mama Elsie said little, her actions made her a role-model of determination and graciousness. She headed off for the third cup of strong coffee to wash away her doubts, and to remain alert for Ming's session.

MING WAS DRESSED in a pale green kimono. Patience was taken aback to see her in a pair of dark-shaded sunglasses. She was struggling with what she was about to reveal. Patience ached, knowing that exposing her emotions was the hardest thing she was about to do. At that moment she felt the struggles Grace went through in harbouring her own pain and fear, for almost two decades.

Ming bowed, lifted her head slowly, eyes searching from behind the heavy shades for a glimpse of Patience in the crowd. She felt a blast of cold wind around her, and looked up at the gigantic air conditioner, hoping it could be turned off. They worked night and day, day after day. The absence of natural light and fresh air, in this extravagant environment, made it necessary that they were never switched off.

'Truth, Understanding and Compassion.' She bowed again, this time with a slight lowering of her head.

'I will share my life-story with you today in the hope that you gain understanding to show compassion to others that have faced similar challenges as I have.'

A whispered, 'Yes,' was uttered in unison.

'I will begin with my grandmother whose life moulded what I do today. Additionally, my mother's life-story in her marriage to my father is important for me to tell, as this shaped my choice to remain single. Traditionally I am labelled a *sheng nu* — a 'left over' woman, but it was my choice to be left over.'

The audience looked at the small figure on the platform, struggling for the courage to share her story as bravely as she could. Everybody was still as questions surfaced in their minds on what had stolen the light from Ming's childhood, and how she became such a gracious woman.

'My grandmother was promised and contracted to a family in marriage by her parents. I say 'to a family' because she *did* not have a say on who her life partner would be. She lived in her husband's family home, serving their every need. Her outlet from the life she did not choose was her poetry writing. She wrote hundreds of poems under the darkness of night. One night her mother-in-law found her sitting outside, writing in the light of a dim candle. That put an end to the only freedom she had.' Ming cleared her throat and continued.

'Nine months after her marriage, she was cursed with the birth of my mother.'

The women gasped at this unexpected description of her mother's birth.

'My beautiful mother, *jia,mu* was a curse because she was not a son.'

Audra shuffled her feet next to Patience, her sudden, uncontrolled, 'Lord, have mercy,' outburst, made Ming stop and smile in her direction. She bowed in acceptance of Audra's shock.

'Yes, only a male heir made a new mother worthy. My *wai-pu* was despised for bearing a female child. My grandmother's life was in danger, she could be killed — infanticide was the norm then. With the blessing of her breast milk, she fled with the assistance of the gardener, it takes one soul to understand and show compassion. He was an elderly man who took great pity on my grandmother. He let her out the back gate of the property with a small bag of fruit. She could not carry the bag, she was weak from the birth and the increased neglect she faced after my mother was born. Carrying the newborn baby and her weak body to safety was the challenge she was determined to achieve.'

A few moans erupted from the audience. Only women could feel and understand that pain and determination were a struggling mother's only hope for saving her child.

'My grandmother found her way back to her parent's home, she hid in the woods nearby until her father left for work on the fields. When she approached her mother, she did not expect to be told she could not stay at the house. Her mother bathed the baby girl, gave her some rice to eat and told her to go to her old friend in the next village where she would be safe.

Wai-pu left before her father came home that night. She arrived around midnight at the home of a welcoming, elderly woman. The next morning she realised the woman was blind. She stayed for more than ten years, indoors, during the day, avoiding detection. The old woman died when my mother was eleven years old. During these years my grandmother picked up her poetry writing again, on her struggles and little joys.'

Ming paused, took a sip of water and slowly removed her sunglasses. Her head remained bowed. She was still uncomfortable to look anyone in the eye. Patience knew the feeling, Ming struggled with the shame of her situation, just like she did, when culture intruded, attempting to alter her life path.

'My grandmother lived in safety at the house until my mother got married. I was born when my mother was seventeen years old.' An applause acknowledged Ming's birth but feared that she too was a female first child.

Akanya could not contain her silence any longer, she whispered rather loudly.

'There's more, you know, she said her mother was the reason she chose not to marry. Dear God, what did her mother do to her?'

'No,' Audra hissed, 'she said the marriage, not her mother, in particular, made her take this decision.'

'Quiet now, let her finish!' Patience said.

Ming bowed in humble acceptance of the applause.

'My mother lived with domestic violence, my father beat her almost every day. I slept in the same room and could hear the abuse while I pretended to be asleep. Slaps, thuds, a whiplash and more. My mother did not make a sound nor cry out in pain during those nights of abuse, for fear she would disturb my sleep.' Ming stopped, reliving those terrible days.

'One night we ran away to our new lives in Shanghai. My mother worked night and day in a clothing factory to ensure I had a home and got an education. She told me I had to be my own person, no man was to dictate the course of my life. She passed away six months before I arrived here at the mission. Her death was the trigger for signing up to the mission's offer.'

Silence and wide-eyed stares looked at the tiny, inclining frame before them.

'I am currently working to get my grandmother's poems published next year with the title, 'Songs of a Stolen Heart.' I know it will bring great comfort to those struggling in similar situations. Much goes unreported about that today. I am still struggling with my identity, and have thrown myself into helping young women overcome their life challenges through my teaching. I am married to my job and the community I serve.' She bowed three times.

'Thank you for listening and cheering me on. I have tried to include everything, but am happy if you have questions for me, just not today, please. I would like to be excused, if possible Masuyo, I feel very tired.

Masuyo put her arm around Ming and walked out with her.

22

REVELATION

A change in plans in the daily schedule at the mission came as an unexpected note slipped under each apartment door. It announced a meeting in the main auditorium at 10 am that morning.

The usual excitement and salivating over what was on offer for breakfast was noticeably absent as groups gathered in earnest conversation. Those who arrived later to breakfast felt uneasy, thinking perhaps they missed something important. In a place where much was revealed, much was also hidden.

Morgan Smith walked up to Patience and Ming hoping they would have knowledge on the agenda of this unscheduled meeting.

'Truth, Understanding and Compassion to you ladies, I trust you had a good night.'

'Yes, thank you, Morgan. I had a better night, slept like a baby. How about you?'

'I can't say the same, I was awake at 2 am and heard the faint sound when the note was slipped under my door. Curiosity got the better of me, so I picked it up and lay pondering until sunrise about what the meeting might entail.'

'Mmmm... two o' clock seems to be the mission's closed doors activity time.' Patience stopped herself from going any further, she knew it might lead to her saying something she might later regret. It was becoming difficult to keep her helicopter discovery private.

'I hope Alva is not ill again, we haven't seen her since the last announcement that she might be sent home.' Ming surmised.

'I doubt it!' Patience barked, losing her grip for a second.

Ming sensed Patience's edginess, she knew better not to ask questions in the company of others.

'We're all in the dark so it's a wait and see game. There's Akanya, let's see what insider information she might have,' Ming suggested.

All attempts to gain Akanya's attention failed to penetrate through her engrossed conversation with Audra. Her swooping arm gestures suggested she was philosophising about something or the other.

'Let's walk over to them, I need to know what to expect today.' Morgan chirped.

Morgan's calm, composed disposition was no different to the person they met last week. Nothing at the mission had changed. How could she think they could make sense of what was happening? No information apart from TUC philosophy was available to them.

Patience was aware that Judd's visit was a decoy to create a sense that they were not really disconnected from the outside world. She knew she would have to tell Ming, at some point, about the departing helicopter. She wondered if the helicopter was housed at the mission or had flown in from somewhere.

Akanya waved for them to come over when she caught sight of them.

'No doubt we are all guessing why this meeting was called. Do you think, it's to tell us to pack our bags to leave?' Her wide-eyed animated face and relentless bobbing head conveyed her hard to miss desire to be home again.

'Hey, wishful thinking, all our thoughts for sure!' Patience laughed.

'Well, you never know in here, it goes from structured to ad hoc at the drop of a hat. I'm keeping hope alive!' Her sudden exaggerated hand gesture on the word 'drop' had them all looking at the ground before they relaxed. Akanya was, after all, the queen of animated hand gestures.

'Politics, my dear Akanya, it's about power and control. Springing the unexpected is the way to keep us cowering and perhaps submissive. My basic History 101 lesson for today!' Morgan added this thought with a glint in her eye, suggesting she was used to this power and control scenario.

'We are held in suspense, believing that we are on a humanitarian mission when clearly there's a political agenda.' Audra added, ignoring Morgan's comment.

'Truth, Understanding and Compassion have never been the values of politicians, so the final outcome will be an interesting one, don't you think?' Ming asked.

Small groups continued their earnest conversations on the state of things at the mission.

At ten o' clock everybody was seated in a subdued pensive mood.

Alexis and Xandria appeared to be running this meeting. They stood to attention, each holding a microphone. Masuyo had not been seen for two days, questions on her whereabouts were met with how busy she was and speculations on whether she was ill.

Xandria welcomed everyone.

'Truth, Understanding and Compassion to you all. We have gathered here this morning to celebrate the tremendous value gained from the personal revelation sessions. To honour this and to confirm that as women we are most compassionate when we are vulnerable, I give you Zuri who will share her story with you. It is hoped what she is about to reveal will assist you in your work with women in the outside world. Without further ado, here's Zuri.'

Patience felt that the hype of the announcement was inappropriate. It created a preconception that Zuri's story was perhaps unworthy of attention, or on the other hand, better than the others that were heard. Or it could be a lack of appropriate marketing if that is what Xandria lacked.

ZURI at just twenty-two years old had endeared herself into the hearts of the older women, with her quiet disposition, only speaking when she was spoken to. Some questioned what she could offer them, let alone teach them when she had not had much life experience.

Zuri's radiant smile calmed the unease. The house lights were down with one spotlight on Zuri's face, the rest of the space was an artificial night. Patience squirmed again at the theatrical effect akin to Shakespeare's dramatised soliloquies. She was cynical when she felt authenticity was lacking.

After her TUC salutation, Zuri began.

'You probably think what does a twenty-two-year-old know about life? My story is no different to those we have already heard, but I believe it needs to be told to show you we are no different. I was born a prison child.'

Silence.

'I was born in prison because my mother was on trial for murder.'

She paused, letting the thought sink in. She looked around the room, confident, comfortable with what she was revealing.

'I am alive, by good grace to share my story. My mother was eighteen when I was born. She waited out the entirety of her pregnancy in prison, and ten more years until we were both released from prison because of her good behaviour. I grew up an inmate in a women's correctional facility, knowing nothing else but regimentation, a half-full belly, coarse language, and my mother's love.' She paused, wanting her words to stick, making the moment last while also catching her breath.

'The highlight of my day was having a teacher come in to teach me Mathematics, Science, and English, every day from the age of three. I loved the books we read in English, it took me to faraway places, removing the unpleasantness of my immediate surroundings. I excelled in Maths and Science too. I am truly grateful to that one teacher, along with my mother, who gave me the best childhood, allowing me to find my way through their guidance. The values gained, propped me up for life's encounters and taught me appropriate reactions. Some of my life lessons were also drawn from repentant women whose crimes did not deserve the 'low-life' label that society imposed upon them. These are the women who did not have the support of this mission or the organisations you run to keep women safe, educating them and preparing them for life's hardships. They were broken women, full of remorse for their actions, biding their time to earn back the life that was taken from them, countless times. It was during this time I learned to fear authority and the power that came with authority. I was in adult company overhearing the abuse these women faced in their homes, and then saw first-hand how they were treated by prison authorities.'

She picked up the bottle of water from the table beside her, took a generous sip, looked up at the audience, feeling sure she was connecting with each of them.

'In all this time, my mother nurtured a gentle soul she knew was essential, if I was to find my place in the world, outside the prison walls. 'Be strong,' she said, 'but always be kind and gentle.' I grew up hearing this and still hear it here today.'

A ripple of sighs signalled relief that Zuri's mother might well be alive today.

'Getting back into mainstream society was the most difficult thing to do, I had no idea what society was like and my mother had to move to another state to avoid the abuse she was receiving for being a 'murderess.' The stigma of being labelled a 'prisoner' or child of a 'murderer' is more difficult to endure than prison life itself. You too, will have a head full of questions on what she did, who was she accused of killing, and for what reason.'

Lots of nodding heads suggested they were with her on this. The tale had to plunge further into darkness for a cathartic cleansing.

'My mother was born into a lower socio-economic family in Britain. Her parents worked for a wealthy parliamentarian at the time. My grandmother was the housekeeper and nanny to her master's children. Two girls and a boy. My mother was fortunate to receive the generosity of her parents' employer, she went to the same elite private school his children attended. Their parents led busy lives, cavorting from one holiday destination to the next, and entertained international governmental officials on a grand scale at the house. My grandmother was the mother the children knew and loved.'

Confused faces in the audience did not know where this was leading to. To them, it seemed like a fortunate life for all.

'I will not mention the name of the family my grandparents worked for, but know some of you might remember this story through the media's slant on the events of one night in particular. The media, to this day, will skew a story for the ratings.'

A round of applause from the mid-section of the auditorium confirmed this universal truth.

'One night there was a house party for visiting diplomats. My grandmother put the children to bed and had my mother help her with odd jobs in the kitchen.

At around ten forty-five that night, my mother was asked to check on the children in the upstairs bedroom, and to report back to her mother before she went off to bed.

When my mother did not return after an hour, my grandmother decided to check if she had fallen asleep.

My seventeen-year-old mother was accosted by one of the visiting delegates when she left the children sleeping in their bedroom. She was shoved into the room adjacent to the children's bedroom.

When my grandmother walked past to check on why my mother had not returned, she heard the shattering of glass and hid behind a wall in the hallway. After a few seconds, my mother dashed out with blood splatters on her clothes, face and hands.

The man who grabbed her on the corridor forced himself on her in his drunken state. He was a local parliamentarian who had been watching her after every glass of whiskey he downed that night. He followed her, and waited outside the children's bedroom. He pushed her into the adjacent room and threw her on the couch where he molested her. She grabbed a table lamp and whacked him on the back of his head. In his drunken state and with the blow to the head, he rolled off her onto shards of broken glass. My distressed mother pierced him in the jugular with a shard of glass, and ran out the room.

My grandmother grabbed her as she ran out, dazed, confused and crying. The police arrived and took my mother away, refusing to hear her end of the situation. She was accused of coercing the man into the bedroom for favours and payment. She was to them, a mere child of a servant.

Nine months later I was born, the child of sin and shame.

Ten long years later, we were released from prison. My mother worked hard to give me the best she could. She could never return to the house, and in those ten years while we were locked away, her parents passed on, leaving her with no family but me. I am a constant reminder of how her life was taken from her, yet never did she ever make me feel unloved or unwanted.'

The spotlight beside Zuri flicked and brought Masuyo into the light. She had been standing right there beside Zuri, in darkness.

'This is my mother, Masuyo.'

The women rose in an endless round of applause, shock clearly evident in all their faces.

Masuyo hugged her daughter and raised her hand in acknowledgement of the applauding women. They left the room, not a word more was said.

Xandria dismissed the ladies, saying they had the afternoon to relax in the pubs or coffee shops in the mission building. Much was in their heads and on their lips that day.

23

GLOBAL ISSUE

A peaceful, contemplative mood resided in the mission with each united in the pain of their yesterdays and glory of promising tomorrows.

Masuyo's revelation through her daughter added to the satisfaction that the mission had no hidden agendas.

Patience's doubts crept in after Alva's unspoken departure. Her memory of the departing helicopter lingered. The truth set them free, they understood each other and felt compassion lighting up their interactions. TUC values had proven to be the fuel for harmonious existence, yet she still felt uneasy with what she knew. She mulled over the complexity of human thought and emotion — the unfamiliar, the place that was not quite home, created doubts that were hard to dispel. The conundrum of life, seek satisfaction when imperfection abounds in supposed perfection. She had to accept that the positives outweighed the negatives at the mission.

THE SCHEDULE for the day was unchanged, no surprise notes left under doors. A day of rotating around venues would provide valuable information on the areas in the world in dire need of further sister intervention. Human trafficking, child labour, child marriages, and sexual abuse earmarked modern slavery as pervasive. All sessions required mandatory attendance, with groups of no more than twenty-five in attendance at each venue. Patience preferred smaller groups, it gave her the opportunity to study her newfound peers at close range.

A whole group meeting in the main auditorium shed light on the dangers of silence and the need to speak up and act to save lives. The realisation that twenty-one million people in almost every country were enslaved, was a startling fact. Exponential work had to be done for emotionally bankrupt young women with no self-esteem, believing they deserved to be treated the way they were. The testimonies leading up to this day had been planned to expose the rawness of mistreatment up close, before diving into the international arena to make a difference. The mission mindset perpetuated a programmed approach that exposure to suffering, would yield rational thinking, to enable specific action needed in each identified location.

The first round of countries demarcated included the Congo, India, Mexico, China and Pakistan. Many more were scheduled for discussion in the days ahead. Each attendee had a booklet to reflect on their thoughts, reactions and ideas for how to work towards ending global human abuse. The session on Pakistan was a self-guided documentary with computers and headphones. Each session was timed at an hour and a half with half an hour for questions and completing reflections.

Patience was surprised to see Akanya heading the session on India's women's struggles. Ming was equally surprised.

'Strange that Akanya did not mention that she was commissioned to showcase the ills of her own country.' Patience said.

'I suppose, in a way it makes sense if it's her country, but the element of subjectivity is the danger, and besides this would have been planned before we arrived here.'

'Mmmm... I agree Akanya is a dark horse at times.'

'Something I have learnt here,' Ming added, 'is that 'truth' is a subjective word.'

'She might have been asked to remain mum, but there are too many instances that make me feel she is an 'insider,' if you know what I mean.'

'Yeah, she is garrulous at the best of times, and secretive when she chooses to be, or perhaps is instructed to be.'

Patience cast off doubts on Ming's perception of 'truth' at the mission. Inwardly she cringed, knowing her speculation on Alva's departure was festering in silence.

Akanya played a ten minute excerpt from a documentary. Text flashed across the screen: *Six hundred and fifty million women. A major Human Rights issue around the world. Seeing is believing.*

Statistics revealed enforced marriages, imprisonment in the family home, body shame, and silence as the enemies of change. The voice-over cited that the inability to speak up propagated a heinous system of protracted abuse. Mothers turned a blind eye, shaming daughters for lying about abuse, daughters were beaten for being non-compliant. Ignorance and silence were condoned as virtuous. Terror, pain and hardship, hauntingly told their own story, visible in the eyes of young victims who were owned by, and subjected to the abuse of modern slavery. Growing shock and whispered voices echoed the horror of what was hidden from global eyes. Patience believed that selective indifference from higher-ups perpetrated modern slavery. While much was done, much was also ignored.

Akanya opened the floor for questions. Patience was deep in thought, this was all too familiar to her. Tribal abuse of African women mirrored the plight of Indian women. She trembled, forcing herself to stop her thoughts travelling back in time. She saw Petros' face, embedded in the recesses of her own pain, a young man who lost his life to set her free. Deep down, it was his selfless act that led to her SHSO initiative, and to the mission. The mission got that right, selfless acts led to successive acts of selflessness.

Akanya explained that the enforced marriages and rape culture were being addressed but had a long way to go before it was obliterated. Too many young women in rural areas had no access to resources and assistance — their cases were unknown, unreported and growing in numbers. Her own life story, revealed a few days earlier, exposed how vulnerable women were in her country.

Audra raised her hand.

'How is it that in a land of spiritual piousness, where religious figures abound, that rapes and beatings occur? I don't get it?'

A tense hush presided in that moment. 'It's the patriarchy, male power that created an insurmountable gender inequality. It has nothing to do with religion, spirituality, or piousness. The scriptures do not teach abuse of women, quite the contrary. Abuse is a social construct, laden with the desire to overpower. Overpopulation and poverty feed this mentality.' Akanya's rigid body broke out in a sweat, her elaborate hand gesticulations were absent. She knew religions of the east were misinterpreted in the west as typical of money grabbing priests. She had to expose modern slavery against women while remaining honest in her allegiance to her country, and in dispelling the myth around eastern spirituality. Audra would demand answers, her impatience was a known characteristic.

'Surely the great spiritual leaders can spread the message that rape and beatings are sinful and shameful acts.'

'The good leaders are powerless, little voices in the wilderness. Criminals think they are greater than God so what hope is there? We need foreign assistance to work with the NGO's and other organisations to stop this now. We have to empower women as we have been, and now with the training at the mission we will be more effective in bringing change for our sisters.'

Patience raised her hand, 'I agree we cannot blame a system of government, religion, and everything in between. We have the voice and capacity to reach out, and we have an obligation to lift our sisters up by equipping them with the skills to walk away, and to be equipped to fend for themselves. It's imperative as an immediate resolution to this heinous crisis'

A round of applause angered Audra.

'Each country should set their own internal parameters and work hard to rectify matters, there's enough going on in the world that each country has to deal with. Each should tend the weeds in their own backyards.'

One, unfamiliar voice called out from the back of the room.

'As an American, that's hypocritical. America's uninvited interference in all matters political around the world, particularly in struggling nations, is endemic. On women's issues, it's unacceptable to lend a helping hand? How do you reconcile this way of thinking with the role you signed up for here?'

Audra cringed with the next round of applause, her bloated beetroot-red face was hard to conceal.

Patience sensed mounting tension, she jumped up.

'We are on a common mission to uplift and lead our struggling sisters to hopefully make a difference in the world of tomorrow. If I may be so bold as to say, India's issues while being addressed internally, needs support, global back-up to stop this uncontrolled abuse of women. This day will reveal that this is not only an Indian issue, I implore an open mind, and yes, to understand is paramount to being compassionate.'

Audra felt the pressure to reply.

'I am not speaking for America, it is solely my opinion that spirituality and abuse are incomprehensible.'

Akanya shook her head in large circular motions, not her

usual dancing, bobbing head. Her vehemence was obvious. She waited for the buzz to die down.

'Have you looked around, churches are denigrated, priests dragged through judicial systems for abuse of young people, numerous acts that have been swept under a rug for decades. Spirituality must not be confused with social issues, human choices lead the individual to commit awful misdeeds. My intention is not to reduce this to, 'my country,' 'your country,' 'my religion' 'your religion' — this is the very mentality that led to the last two world wars, and we are sitting on the brink of a third. Who are victims of such a male mindset? Our girls, our women, our babies? Whatever race, creed, or religion, women need united global attention and assistance to stop this to save them NOW!'

Her words reverberated with a force nobody had expected. The maternal, calm demeanour of the past few months had disappeared in her passion to be heard and understood in conveying her country's truth. She was a woman on a steadfast mission and beware the person who tried to stop her!

Country, after country in each of the groups, revealed a similar pattern of abuse. Congo, China, Pakistan, Mexico and more.

Heated clashes abated. Strategies were discussed, action plans set up with what might be possible in some countries and what would need a different approach in others. By the end of the strategy sessions, an emotionally drained group of women walked into the auditorium for Masuyo's wrapping up of the day.

'Today, Truth, Understanding and Compassion took another leap forward. Argument is good if it leads to constructive working towards the ills facing our sisters. Learning to listen to each other is what we all have to take into the world as valuable, for transition in the communities we serve. Victim or leader is of no consequence when it comes to listening, to understand and communicate what is just and essential. This will save lives. In this mission, we are our own united nations. We are global citizens. Fear not the coming of the new dawn, my sisters, you have the power to change tomorrow!'

Every eye was fixed on Masuyo. Her intensity ran as deep as Akanya's. Patience acknowledged that strength and aggression were opposing forces. Strength, standing on the shoulders of compassion held the promise of a better world.

24

FELICITY STRIKES AGAIN

Grace returned to ER a week later. That afternoon she contemplated whether she should wear her engagement ring to work.

She stepped out onto the balcony. The late afternoon sun sparkled off her generous diamond. The colours glittered in a spiral gyration as she twirled her hand, playing to the sunlight.

She pulled off the ring, feeling guilty for this indulgent, girlish moment. She knew Keefe would understand that it was impossible to wear her ring on duty. She gently wrapped it in its soft red silk cloth. A lump rose in her throat, Patience would have squealed with delight at the sheer size of the stone, and taken endless photographs — she was the queen of bling. Her mother would have been planning the wedding from the moment she heard of their engagement. She ached to have them beside her, laughing, loving and planning...

She began writing her thoughts ever since Patience disappeared. Her therapist had advised her to start journaling her past trauma for the therapeutic healing that came with writing. She wrote a conversation with Patience.

I finally did it, sis, I kept him hanging on like you said. He waited. I said yes! I won't marry him without you. He knows it. You better get back for Keefe's sake!

She scribbled an image of the ring and closed the book. She closed her eyes, trying to imagine where Patience was, hoping she could feel the shared psychic connection they had as children. In recent months, since Patience was reported missing, Grace had taken to talking to herself, to still her anxiety during her moments of solitude. She got into the car mouthing, 'I know you will be back.'

ANDREW LANG SMILED with every tooth visible when he saw Grace walk through ER's sliding doors. He approached her with outstretched arms, swooping her in a bear-hug.

'Congratulations Grace! I'm so happy you made the commitment. Keefe must be over the moon. Now, where's that rock?'

'Thank you, Andrew, I can't wear it on duty, it would be cumbersome and could injure the patients when I'm scurrying around when we get hectic in here.'

Andrew's crinkled nose and a twinkle in his eye told her he had an uncontrollable boyish thought.

'What is it, just say it! I won't be offended.'

'Must be quite a rock, hey. I'm imagining a tabloid headline, 'City Hospital ER Medic Throwing Rocks' or some such bizarre headline. Sorry, Grace, my silly sense of humour.'

'Stop! Now, I will never wear my ring on duty, I'm scarred for life with that headline!'

They shared a crazy laugh that came with old friendship. The closeness between them helped Grace during her anxious times.

'Well Dr Lang, enough merriment for one night, we better prepare for the evening ahead.'

S{HE FLICKED} through her text messages, two unread messages from Felicity Cassano loomed on her phone. She was stopping over in Sydney en route to The Hague to address the missing aircraft and to initiate further action on the whereabouts of its passengers. Felicity had a knack of elevating Grace's anxiety with her harsh, critical opinions and trite text messages. Deep down she knew she appreciated that Felicity was dead-set on finding Patience. The last line in the message commanded, *Call me. I need more information.*

Another level of anxiety was telling Felicity that she and Keefe were engaged. She had to be prepared for a jab or two on doing this while poor Patience was in trouble. Several deep breaths were always needed when Felicity was in town.

M{UCH TO} G{RACE'S DISAPPOINTMENT}, Felicity booked an overnight stopover in Sydney before heading to The Hague. She asked Grace to meet her for dinner to discuss the latest on Patience's situation. Grace asked if she could bring Virginia Bale along to which she received a categorical 'no' and words on how ridiculous it was to think that the 'girl' could possibly contribute anything to the situation. Grace hated the reference to Virginia as 'girl,' but Felicity's direct, hard-nosed approach was unchangeable. She reserved her tenderness for Patience and her ailing husband, Alf.

Dinner at *Nicks Bar and Grill* was a good idea, it offered a level of protection from the interrogation she would receive from Felicity. At least she would be saved the embarrassment of having to defend herself when questions were fired at her. After all these years of knowing Felicity, she still had the ability to ruffle Grace's feathers. She looked at herself in the mirror, retouched her lipstick and said, *you can do this Grace!*

FELICITY'S HAIR was pinned atop her head, her bright red lipstick and taut jaw meant she was ready for business.

'Hello, Grace, glad you could meet me this evening. Any further news or letters?'

Grace expected the confrontational questions. So much for social niceties, but of course this was a meeting, it was not about her, or friends catching up.

'Hi, Felicity, good to see you. How's Alf doing? No further news, I'm afraid, nothing after Patience's letter.'

'Alf's doing better this week, but it's a see-saw, you just never know. Now let me outline my modus operandi regarding this trip to The Hague. This is an international matter, now that we know a great many women from different parts of the world were on board that flight to God knows where! Many of my personal contacts are keen to assist through their connections with the International Criminal Court, which should give this the attention and support needed. Several meetings are lined up to address the matter. I planned to meet the families and associates of the other missing Australian delegates, but that did not happen, unfortunately. This is why I need you to keep in close contact with me, while I'm away, with any updates from these families.'

She spoke without catching her breath, she was on a mission and nothing was going to stand in her way. Anything that Grace proposed was tossed aside. Felicity had two television interviews in The Hague to get the media spinning their magic, to up the ante on this investigation.

Grace kept her palms crossed on her lap to conceal her engagement ring from sight until the drinks and food arrived.

'Look, Grace, we cannot pussy-foot around this anymore, we need action. The consolation is, at least we know Patience is alive, that is worth fighting for. I hope all passengers are alive and well.'

Grace appreciated Felicity's concern and love for Patience. If anyone could get answers on the situation it would be her.

'How are things going with the girl running the safe houses for Patience? Is she coping?'

'Virginia is coping very well, I don't do much to help her these days. She's managing new staff too. I'm very proud of what she's achieved after her setback.'

'Really? Would not have thought she had one responsible bone in her body with the situation she got herself into, with that layabout boyfriend. She didn't offer much in my last meeting with you both.'

'That's a bit unfair, she's come a long way, we should give her credit for that, and what she's doing for the Sisters Helping Sisters Organisation.'

'Well, what do you know!' True to Felicity form, she dismissed Grace's praise for Virginia. 'Thank goodness, the drinks are here. This place is busy as always.' She took no notice of the smiling waiter, snatched the drink from his hand, and gulped it down, like it was her last drink.

Grace thanked the young man and confirmed their dinner order. She picked up her drink with her right hand, keeping her left hand concealed for a while longer, to buy her more time, before a barrage of questions followed about her engagement.

A few more gulps of her drink, mellowed Felicity's sniping tongue until she asked the dreaded question — Grace had no way out.

'How are things with you and the Irishman?'

'Keefe, his name's Keefe, he's very well thank you. We got engaged in Belfast. His mother is quite ill, he's returning next week. His sister is an attorney too.' There she got it out, everything all at once, staccato style.

'Sorry to hear about Keefe's mother, another legal eagle in our midst, good to know.'

Grace knew this politeness would not last, it was triggered by the expected politeness over Mrs Daly's illness.

'Where's the ring, ahh... you have the left hand tucked away!'

Grace lifted her left hand to Felicity's guffaw, turning a few heads that were out for a quiet romantic dinner. With lightning speed, she put her hand back on her lap.

'Hang on, not so fast! Give me a closer look.'

'Later, it's just a ring.'

'Just a ring, I'll be damned, look at the size of that rock! Congratulations Grace, you earned this. At least your anxieties can be put to rest now!' Another ear shattering guffaw left Grace scarlet-faced.

Grace's anxiety was a well-known fact with Felicity after their girls' weekend at a seaside cottage in Melbourne, over a year ago. She would give anything to erase Felicity's memory of her public breakdown on that fateful weekend together.

'When do you plan to get married?'

'Not now, I won't get married until Patience is back.'

'Yeah, that's the sensible thing to do. May I have a look at the letter, Patience's letter, we've only had a telephone conversation about it.'

She studied the letter, commenting that it was good that it was handwritten. She scrutinised the envelope and postage stamp.

'There's a freshness about the paper and ink which suggests it hasn't been floating around for too long. The letter itself is not dated. That's odd, I know your sister's a stickler for dating every-thing that has her signature appended to it. Odd. But, it appears recent, which is a hopeful sign. I suspect the passengers are not in Singapore as per the date-stamp, because aeronautical reports indicate the aircraft veered off the flight path. My assumption is that the letter was taken to Singapore to be mailed.'

'Why? Is it some sort of decoy to their whereabouts? This makes the whole situation appear rigged which scares me.'

'If anything, Patience has her head screwed on the right way, she would not enter into something if there was a potential threat. She's had experience with her abduction in South Africa.

She has been led by her heart on this venture, but there's no saying there's no danger lurking. Going off the intended flight path is not an act of sabotage, it's not a terrorist act — it was a flight on some humanitarian mission if Patience got on it.'

Felicity was ticking, thoughts emerged on all the possible scenarios. Her eyes darted at the same speed as her emerging thoughts.

'There's something else afoot, I have not quite got my finger on it. Can you think of anything else she might have said that you missed telling me?'

'I've wracked my brain, but nothing new or forgotten comes to mind. She was vague about the venture she embarked on.' Grace felt guilty in admitting that she did not know enough about her sister's trip.

'Yeah, this letter is dressed in generalisations. I need to look at it closely for any clues. I have to take this with me to The Hague?'

'I need a copy of it, Felicity, here let me photograph it as my copy.'

'I will return it to you when I get back, it might help in the investigation.'

The hammering, centralised 'I' made Grace uncomfortable, she was useless and unwanted in the quest to find her sister.

She thanked Felicity for all she was doing. Felicity looked at Grace with a surprising tenderness.

'Like you, I want my girl back. I miss the light she brings into my world man!'

Grace saw a fleeting welling up of Felicity's hard eyes. Her iron-clad will ensured she stopped the floodgates.

She recalled her mother cautioning her to be gentle with Felicity in her aggressive 'I' moments, due to her fractured childhood. Her hidden vulnerability was close to the surface with Alf's illness, and the uncertainty of Patience's whereabouts.

They parted that night with a gentle hug, nothing more was said.

25

SAD NEWS

As fate would have it, Grace received a second letter from Patience, two days after Felicity set off for The Hague. Going to her apartment mailbox, and the drive to her post office box became a daily ritual ever since Patience's last letter arrived. Her promise to stay in touch this way, left Grace longing for the next letter.

She read through it three times, making sure no hidden messages were missed — nothing new was said, just a consoling message indicating she was safe. Her buzzing mobile phone interrupted her reverie to the exciting news that Virginia Bale had also received a letter from Patience that day.

Grace headed off to meet her at the SHSO office in George Street. She was not on shift that night, sleep was not essential. Getting to the heart of each letter was more important.

She entered the building with mixed feelings. It was not the same without Patience's smiling face at the door. What additional news would Virginia's letter have? Would Patience shut her off from details of her whereabouts because of her history with anxiety? Would this exclude her from the truth?

~

VIRGINIA MET her downstairs in the lobby. The building was under renovation, access to the sixth floor was from an unfamiliar east-side stairway.

'Hello Virginia, thank you for meeting me, my sense of direction is hopeless when things change. I might have ended up on the wrong floor!' Grace laughed, adding, 'it's been a while since my last visit, I don't enjoy taking a train into the city, but the lack of parking leaves no option.'

'Hello Grace,' Virginia had recently, after much persuasion, taken to calling Grace by her first name.

'Patience's parking spot is vacant, I take the train in most days. I find sitting in… interminable… traffic, is that the right word… an irritation.' Her hesitant tone was a giveaway that she was still in awe of Grace.

The smiling face of an older woman greeted Grace at the reception desk in the SHSO office.

'Grace, this is Lindiwe Johnson our new staff member,' Virginia announced. She's a godsend with her experience in organisations such as ours — she's from South Africa too.'

'Lovely to meet you. Sorry, I was not around to meet you sooner, I was on a flying trip to Belfast, and had to play catch up when I got back to work.' Grace surprised herself that she spoke to a stranger with such ease. Lindiwe's warmth and radiance made her comfortable. She was in her late fifties, greying around the temples with eyes of experience, confirming Virginia had made the right choice in employing her.

'Good to meet you too. Please don't apologise, Virginia told me how hectic your schedule has been. I am also sorry to hear about the situation with your sister, I pray she returns soon. May I get you a coffee?'

'Thank you for your kind words. Yes please, coffee will be most welcome.'

Grace cast a curious eye around the office. Everything struck her as immaculate, orderly and professional. Files were labelled, colour-coded and sat in neat rows on the bookshelves. The reception desk had a vase with yellow and white roses, Patience's desk had one yellow rose in a small tubular vase. Virginia kept her presence alive in the office.

'Wow, this place looks amazing, you've done a sterling job looking after things for Patience. You've taken so much off my hands too.' Grace chose not to say anything to let her sister down on the organised chaos of her office space. Files and endless mounds of paper sky-scraped her desk, but she knew where everything was at the drop of a hat. Now there was a professional, business atmosphere about the place.

Patience turned everything she touched into a cosy home. Grace felt a tinge of nostalgia at that thought. She was so much like Varuna whose creative chaos in the kitchen produced the most delectable dishes. The kitchen counter strewn with spice jars and a sink with a precarious stack of dishes did not deter her. From all of that seeming chaos during a frenzied Sunday afternoon of cooking, emerged a hedonistic aroma and sight to behold. Delicately spiced, yellow speckled cardamom rice, a rich, dark, reddish gravy with the freshest fish she could find, finished off with a topping of chopped coriander and spring onion had Grace and Patience drooling for a first taste. Memories surfaced, tugging at her heart.

Patience's mother was the complete opposite, a neat freak, who tidied up Varuna's cooking frenzy, smiling as she worked, saying ever so softly, '*eish*, you cook like God is guiding your hand, you should see yourself, mama, like an artist!' Elsie never called Varuna by her first name, when Varuna insisted on her dropping the 'Mrs' address, she was comfortable in the respect 'mama' held for her. Grace was more Elsie's daughter, and Patience was almost an incarnation of Varuna. She had to have her sister back. Her carefree light and spirit was sorely missed, leaving a gaping hole in Grace's life.

Virginia swapped her letter for Grace's letter. They read and reread, searching for clues that they might have missed. Virginia's letter was long. It read:

My dearest Virginia,

How do I even begin to thank you for taking care of the sisters and our humble office? You have my immeasurable thanks.

I cannot give you a clear indication of when I will return. Know that I am safe, with good people and I am well taken care of. I am gaining skills that will help me improve how I serve others in need. Watch over Grace for me, I worry about her worrying over me. My whereabouts have become inconsequential to me, now, although it must be of grave concern to you and Grace. The only thing I want is to be back home with my loved ones, as soon as possible, to ease the burdens I left you to carry. I hope Sprite and Ajax are not too much trouble, I miss them so much. I feel I've deserted my babies, but know how much you and Grace will do to care for them. I will write as often as I can.

I'm enclosing a list of things that require attention at the safe houses, although I suspect you have that under control. Please do not feel any pressure to tick all the boxes. What matters most is that our distressed sisters are safe and receiving the necessary mental, physical and emotional care.

GRACE MADE a mental note of what she would assist Virginia to accomplish.

'She's okay, Grace, I feel it... although I worry about where in the world she might be right now, I'm grateful for her letter. She has an amazing memory and what a glorious childhood you both had together, I feel... I've taken that journey into your childhood through the love you both share. She certainly cherishes your years together. How fortunate you both are!'

Grace absorbed Virginia's words like a parched sponge. She heard the sensitivity and maturity in her voice. She was no longer the lost young woman she met outside the coffee shop, just under a year ago, the one who devoured her ham croissant in a few seconds. Virginia had come a long way. This thought warmed Grace in that she knew Virginia had the potential to be more than her boyfriend had led her to believe.

'I miss receiving photographs of the places Patience would visit and pretend to be a real estate marketer. She would video her hotel room when she was away and talk through the 'state of the art Jacuzzi that offers many pleasurable hours and a heavenly vision of Melbourne's skyline.' Now nothing, I cannot summon my imagination to create the place she might be in...'

'She's safe, Grace, hang onto that.'

Grace stayed on that afternoon to assist Lindiwe and Virginia with paperwork that needed to be completed on the placement of a new recruitment of sisters from across the country.

SHE HURRIED home that evening to call Keefe. Mam was now on life support.

'Hello *mo ghrá,* I was expecting your call earlier in anticipation of hearing what Patience had to say in her letter, after your late night text message.'

Hi Keefe, sorry, I was delayed helping Virginia at the office, she's received a letter too. How is mam doing? How's Aileen holding up?'

'Long story, tell me about Patience's letter first.'

'It's not much different to the first letter except that she is improving her skills as promised when she signed up for the course. Both letters were along the same lines, more consoling us that she was doing well.'

Keefe absorbed everything Grace said, thinking how to couch his thoughts without alarming her.

'She must be under instruction not to say too much. These are handwritten letters when it could be a text message or email, this makes me think there are controls in place on how much she reveals about where she is, and precisely what the course is about. What do you think?'

'Yeah, I feel there must be some pressure. I had a terrifying thought when Virginia mentioned that Patience signed a secrecy clause. I thought, what if she was taken by a terrorist, or some criminal organisation where she might be held hostage for some unknown reason. It certainly feels that way, with this cloak, and heaven forbid dagger communication.'

'Not likely. There is our answer, the secrecy clause. I believe all will be revealed in due course, it has to be some government initiative. Perhaps the plane is housed in a zone where satellite detection cannot penetrate, just my rambling thoughts.' He paused again tossing around thoughts that crept in.

'I don't know what to think, really, it's a confusing state of affairs. I keep questioning why this has happened again in Patience's life. Each thought complicates things further, I have to hang onto the fact that she's alive and her handwriting proves that to me. I have to shake thoughts of a gun being held over her as she writes these letters!' Grace's agitated tone made Keefe edgy. He had to be truthful with her in all his surmising on the situation, but, how much could he really share of his thoughts, when her emotions were achingly raw.

'Aye, I understand *mo ghrá*, this is very difficult for you, but we have to think outside the square. If this is a government initiative, at least there's a semblance of further hope that she is indeed safe.'

'Sorry Keefe, I don't have your trust in governments.' Grace's trite response shut down further speculations.

'All I'm going to say now before I stop is that you must get this latest bit of information from Virginia, on the secrecy clause, to Felicity while she's in The Hague.'

'Yes, I intend to do that today. Please tell me, how are things with mam?'

'Aileen and I are prepared that the end is close, we don't want mam to struggle in pain. No more surgery. We are meeting with mam's parish priest this afternoon for guidance on how to proceed. She is a devout Catholic. Although Aileen and I strayed a bit over the years, we want to honour her in the decision we take, that is best for her. I don't want to make any medical decisions as her son.'

'That's a very thoughtful choice. I'm glad Aileen is there to support you.'

'Aye, always. I'm concerned about your wellbeing, I should be there with you during this stressful time.'

'I'll be fine, we are both facing challenges. Yours is a tough one. I'm grateful for your honest conversations. You give me sensible perspective on things I dare not think about on my own.'

'I need to say, one more thing. If this is indeed a government initiative, and we are perceived as interfering in the process with Felicity's meeting in The Hague, we could be blocked from Patience's communication with us. They might be intercepted. We must tread carefully.'

'Yes, that's a scary thought, it's the stuff I thought I would only see in a movie or read in a spy-thriller. You have a busy day ahead, we'll keep the messages flowing. Pass on my love to Aileen. When you are in quiet conversation with mam, let her know I'm holding her in positive energy.'

'Thank you so much, *mo ghrá*, chat later.'

AT 4 PM BELFAST TIME, Grace received a text message from Keefe.

My dearest mam gave up her struggle at 3.45 pm today while Aileen and I were in consultation with Father Paul. I will call you at 7 am your time. May my dearest mam rest in eternal peace.

26

CALLED TO SERVE

A white envelope sat unnoticed on the entrance mat in Patience's room. The face down envelope caught her eye when she was ready to step out for breakfast — her heart skipped a beat. Could it be by some stroke of divine luck, a letter from Grace? She snatched it off the mat, turned it around, no postage stamp, just her name scrawled on the front. It was a mission message that must have come in during the night.

Frustrated, and disappointed that she was deluding herself that it could be from Grace when she knew her whereabouts were unknown, left her scatty. The last weeks at the mission tested her staying power, she had to see this through, she had come this far. Dreams of being picked up by a helicopter consumed her nights, an escape she was longing for. She had to summon the courage to get her through to the end. Commitment was paramount.

She shut her eyes, opening the envelope, peering at it one eye at a time, denying that she might have to do something that day, a last minute thing, she was exhausted from many sleepless nights.

The officious tone of the note read: *Please meet Masuyo in her private office at nine thirty this morning.* No apology for the late notice. For the first time since her arrival, Patience felt a vaulting and descending churn in the pit of her belly that tested her usual resilience. What was this about with just two weeks left at the mission?

SITTING AT HER DESK, dressed in a white kimono with a silk scarf loosely draped over her head, Masuyo looked angelic and deathly pale.

She rose to greet Patience with her usual calm demeanour.

'Truth Understanding and Compassion to you, Sister Patience. I trust you slept well.'

Patience's guard went up with a resounding thud in her chest. What's with the 'Sister Patience?' She had to still her tongue. Her belly flipped a few more times in a mad dance as she waited for what felt like a jury verdict.

'I slept very well thank you, Truth Understanding and Compassion to you too.' She was unaffected by her white lie. She tossed and turned all night, hearing engines and seeing Grace's face smiling up at her.

'That's good, you're probably confused by this sudden meeting. You have been among our best chosen sisters, invited to join the mission.'

Cut to the chase, don't mess with my head, thumped in her brain, she had the urge to yell, feeling her equanimity sinking with the weight of a truckload of rocks.

Her lips told a different story.

'Thank you kindly.'

In her previous life, she would demand to know what was going on. Three short months in the mission had made her compliant. Was it TUC that had this effect, or had the women of the mission smoothed her edges?

'You recall that countries were to be allocated in the final weeks to those who signed up to serve on the outside?'

'I do, so the time has arrived. Which country have I been allocated?'

She needed the information to mentally prepare herself for a return to mainstream society, which she feared she might have to readjust to.

'After careful consideration, in consultation with our mission HQ, it has been decided that you will be placed in a rural community in Mexico. A group of young women there need to be carried forward in leadership training that you will provide.'

Patience absorbed this, unfazed by the location as her mind buzzed with how she would possibly cope with the language barrier in such a short space of time.

'Do these young women speak English?'

'Some would have a limited ability and others not at all.' She looked at Patience sussing out whether she was ready to jump ship as her cautious questioning suggested.

'Will recruits from this mission be appointed alongside me in this rural community?'

'There are two people already heading the community, you will slip in, pick up the reins and move the women into the next phase of their training. All information will be provided to you within forty-eight hours. Nobody from this group will be with you.'

'Why is that? We've forged great connections through TUC values here. We would be amazing in spreading and developing this in the world if we were paired in our designated communities.'

Masuyo sensed Patience's agitation, she wanted rational answers.

'The mission's policy is to have you in service away from the familiar to maximise the delivery of your strengths in training others in need, with minimum or no social and emotional distractions.'

'I see. Social distractions are forbidden, do we now get to have direct contact with our families? The letters were good, we need voice contact... it has been a long time.'

'You get one telephone call a month to one person in your family, all three calls in total will be to the same person you choose to keep in contact with.'

Patience felt the pressure of those lines like a tightening noose ready to squeeze the last breath from her lungs. She surveyed Masuyo's placid exterior with the alpha tigress brimming beneath.

'Are all ladies being informed of their placements today?'

'You are the first, there will be staggered sessions throughout the day. By dinner, all who signed up will know where they are going to serve. I appeal to you to keep your placement to yourself until we are ready to announce to all.'

'Certainly, always. Will I get any information to read? I'm eager to get my head around things now that I know my role and where I'm placed.'

'Xandria will bring a folder to you, later tonight, for your perusal. Specific details will only be handed over in forty-eight hours as mentioned.'

Patience departed, perplexed by Masuyo's officious manner — she knew she could never emulate this disposition. She was born to be a social butterfly. She ran her SHSO as a friendly organisation where hierarchy was non-existent. Masuyo sent out mixed signals, the strong, controlling woman, and the affable, vulnerable woman at other times. Was this the type of leadership that the mission expected? Was this the mission's vision for how women should lead the world of tomorrow?

Later that day, Audra sidled up to Patience, eager for a quiet word.

'Truth, Understanding, and Compassion to you, Patience, may I have a quick word. Everybody seems to be preoccupied today.'

'What's on your mind, Audra?' She knew Audra was either allocated a country, or had word that the process was in motion.

'I've noticed a lot of the ladies going in the direction of Masuyo's office. I have an appointment at four o' clock but have no idea what it's about. Nobody is available to talk to me about this. Those going in, disappear before I can get to them.'

Xandria and Alexis appeared out of nowhere.

'Anything the matter ladies?' Xandria asked.

Audra's was taken aback by the unexpected intrusion. Her surprise was hard to conceal, her flushed beetroot face, frenzied darting looks at Patience, and her silence was a dead giveaway that she was stressed. She fumbled, trying to respond.

'No... everything is... we were chatting about how fast the three months have sped by, and we will have to readjust when we get home...' Her pleading eyes begged Patience to intervene as she struggled to stop herself descending into a stuttering mess. Audra had moments when her feisty spirit emerged, in recent weeks, after her personal testimony, she displayed more inconsistent patterns of behaviour, slipping between fear and being brazen.

'Yes, we were talking about how we would get back to what we were doing before we arrived here. I was telling Audra I was away for an additional three months before I came to the mission. Audra is surprised I've been away for that long.' Patience felt the flush in her cheeks, the white lie flowed with no guilt attached. She felt the overwhelming need to protect Audra in this fragile moment.

'We'll leave you to it then, it's surprising how much we learn about each other every day.' Alexis laughed as they moved away to join another group, deep in conversation.

'Phew! Thank you, Patience, I lost it there. You saved my skin.'

'Look, Audra, you must calm down and trust the process. You will have your answer by four o' clock today, enjoy the time left here. Stop stewing over things. This has been quite an educative experience, you must agree.'

Patience had promised she would not talk about her placement, she felt awful withholding this from Audra, it was necessary — Audra would not keep a lid on it, she had to protect her integrity. The last thing she wanted was to invite negative attention, especially from Masuyo, who could warm and chill a person in the same instant. She steered the conversation to tepid waters.

'What workshop are you attending next?'

'The 'Teaching Confidence' session with young Zuri. She is an amazing young woman. I admire her selflessness for one so young, and her dedication to her mother. Are you in the same workshop?'

'I'm in the research library later, your session will be great.'

'Oh, what are you researching?'

Patience thanked her lucky stars when Deidre and Akanya joined them. She could not bear another white lie today. She was beginning to agree with Ming's issue with 'truth' at the mission! It was almost as if it was a divide and rule strategy, tell someone something, and then tell them not to tell others, when the information was to become public knowledge anyway. Was this a test of their integrity?

AKANYA'S ROUND, beaming face, and booming voice conveyed her infectious happiness.

'Two weeks! Can you believe just two weeks and we'll be homeward bound.' She shot her arms skyward to mimic a departing aircraft, or perhaps a rocket launching into space.

Patience wondered whether she had pulled out of the additional three months of community service. Audra clammed up around Akanya in recent weeks. Mistrust crept into their relationship ever since she presented the segment on India and the state of the nation regarding women in rural communities.

Audra perceived it as a privilege granted to Akanya. She brooded over whether she was really 'one of them.'

It was admirable that Akanya was either oblivious to Audra's hostility, or one who moved on after a disagreement.

'I noticed your name booked in for the 'Teaching Confidence' session, Audra, I'm booked in it too, it should be interesting, don't you think?'

Audra mumbled, 'I trust Zuri so I'm happy to accept whatever she offers.'

Akanya laughed, her sweeping, circular hand gesture accompanied, 'everybody can be trusted in here. We are in paradise!'

Nobody responded to the comment.

Deidre said she was doing the 'Do's and Don'ts for mission Women'

Patience climbed in to subvert the brewing tension Audra was hell-bent on fanning.

'Take copious notes, I'd love to know how that is defined. I might be breaking a few rules on that, for sure!'

Audra excused herself from the group. Akanya's large, curious eyes followed Audra as she walked away.

'Is Audra okay? She was unusually quiet, is something the matter?' She looked at Patience for an answer.

'Not that I am aware of, sorry Akanya.' Patience cringed as the series of white lies accrued with rapidity in less than an hour.

EACH HEADED off to their respective workshops. Patience was eager to research as much as she could on female culture in rural

Mexico. She was keen to learn a few things every day, greeting, welcoming Mexican phrases and other social niceties.

Nobody was prepared for the reactions of some, regarding where they were to be placed as mentors.

27

CHANGES

Silence was clouded by an uneasiness that night. Audra, and Akanya were absent from dinner. Patience waited to hear the outcome of the final country placements as Masuyo had promised — Zuri and Masuyo were nowhere in sight.

Guarded reservation between Ming and Patience was noticeable in their lack of laughter and flowing conversation. Each held back sharing the outcome of their meeting on the country they were allocated. Both were bound by Masuyo's verbal secrecy request.

Secrecy whittled away trust in growing relationships. Patience knew for all the good the mission was doing, some of its strategies were counterproductive to social engagement — the secrecy annoyed her. She was close to breaching it, her friendship with Ming was worth saving.

Ming retreated into her shell, uncomfortable and guilty with the secret imposed upon her.

Patience witnessed the corrosive collapse of her sister's world, after their mother's death. Varuna went to her grave with no knowledge of her daughter's hidden pain. At that moment,

Patience knew that the mission's unwritten secrecy code had to be addressed. It was eroding morale and destroying relationships. She had no answer on how this could be achieved without overstepping the mission's expectations.

Secrecy had to be cremated, not buried, for trust to survive.

'Truth, Understanding and Compassion to you, Ming. Did you have a restful night?'

'The same to you, Patience. Thanks, yes I did.'

Open and shut. Her obvious avoidance of the traditional TUC greeting signalled her struggle. Patience was not going to hold back if there was a compromising of truth, she was going to call it, expose it, and destroy it!

'You don't look like you had a good night. We need to talk.'

Ming's tea-cup rattled as her tense, unsteady hands placed it on the saucer.

'I know we can't talk in here, Alexis and Xandria are on the prowl, it's obvious their radar is primed for some reason. My class is not until ten o' clock, how about you? We could take a stroll into the greenhouse, that's a quiet, unobtrusive location.'

'I don't have a class, I'm doing some research in the media centre,' Ming whispered.

Both had no appetite that morning, a hot drink was all they could stomach. Alexis stopped at their table, with a message that a meeting with Masuyo was scheduled for two o' clock that afternoon.

The greenhouse was as close to the outdoors as they would get. Patience stopped to inhale the familiar scent of roses, Ming touched the carrots, and bent over to cradle the tomatoes — they needed the freshness of the natural world.

'How odd that we have a meeting together with Masuyo?'

'Something's up, I smell it a mile away. Look at us, we are a picture of misery. We have to safeguard what matters to us. This secrecy is destructive, I can't handle this change. I'm not sure I can hold this in much longer,' Patience lamented.

'I know what you mean, but can we please wait until after our meeting before we talk further on this?'

Patience was unsure of Ming's intention, she had a momentary, fearful thought that Ming was now part of the 'insider' group. Why did she want to defer this discussion? In all her desire to be free of secrecy and lies, she was forced to comply.

'Whatever you want, my friend. Just one question, do you have any idea what's happened to Audra and Akanya?'

'I have noticed their absence, who wouldn't, they are larger than life personalities in here. I have no information on them.'

Patience toyed with the thought that, they too, might have slipped out by helicopter, while the mission slept.

'Ah, well I suppose in time things will be unveiled, as they do.'

They left for their ten o'clock class and research. Everyone they passed along the way was silent, their eyes avoiding an invitation to talk. TUC was hidden from all lips.

THREE MONTHS ago they arrived to a clinical world. Diverse personalities colourised the space they inhabited, making it bearable. Now a locked mentality infiltrated their personal space with each other.

TUC was essential for human survival and harmony, but a nagging doubt resurfaced.

THEY ARRIVED SEPARATELY to their joint two o' clock meeting. Masuyo appeared distracted, shuffling through papers on her desk. Her black kimono added years to her fine-lined forehead.

'Truth, Understanding, and Compassion sisters. Thank you for being punctual. I will try not to take too much of your time as you have much to prepare for in your new roles. A situation arose late yesterday that needs to be rectified today. HQ awaits my paperwork on this. I will present you with fresh options.'

Ming's lowered head, slipped an inch lower as her anxiety rose in anticipation of the changes being suggested. Was she to be castigated to some god-forsaken location?

Patience thought, spit it out sister, this is killing us.

'Sister Audra is unhappy with her placement and has had quite a negative reaction. My thoughts are to swap placements around for a harmonious transition into your roles.'

Patience bit her tongue after she said it.

'Out with it please, what will you have us do now?'

A faint smile swept over Masuyo's lips.

'I like your forthright attitude, sister.'

Ming looked up, preparing herself for this verdict.

'Where is Audra placed?' Patience asked.

'The mission has placed her in Pakistan?'

'What reason does she offer for not wanting to go there?'

'The thing is she's not unhappy about the location, it's more about Akanya's placement.'

This slippery, lathering, roundabout way of releasing information, drop by drop, irked Patience. Masuyo was known for her directness, now she was crawling around the point like every politician, or a new driver trying to parallel-park for the first time.

'Ok, where is Akanya placed?'

'India.'

Ming shot Patience a knowing look before reverting to her bowed pose.

'To be honest, I can understand why Audra is upset, yes, she would want to be placed in the United States.'

She was not prepared to shut her up on the injustice that was clearly at work.

'Can you elaborate on why you say this?' Masuyo asked with glaring agitation.

'I might like to be placed in Australia, close to my sister, and

I'm sure Ming would want the same if she was not placed in China.'

'Ming has been placed in the Congo — you confirm my justification that you two are the most trusted recruits.'

That bit of flattery left them unmoved if it was meant to be a compliment.

'How did Audra get wind of Akanya's placement?'

Patience wanted the whole story, she detested bite-size bits of information.

'They were the reason for my request to keep your locations to yourselves until it was finalised. These two have proved they cannot caution their tongues at the best of times.' Masuyo's tone was ruffled by the tension this situation had created.

'This is why you were called in today. Ming, you will be moved to India and Audra will be moved to the Congo. Akanya will go to Mexico and you,' she smiled at Patience, 'will go to Pakistan.'

Ming and Patience were silent at this deliberate chessboard manoeuvre.

'I approached you both in this situation because you are perceived as the sensible recruits. I apologise for these unplanned changes. I have to finalise this with HQ today, to get the ball rolling in settling you in those locations.'

'Yes, I will accept Pakistan.'

Masuyo's shoulders dropped with relief.

'Thank you, sister.'

Ming nodded, 'I accept the change too. I don't think we have an option in the matter.'

Patience's heart sang with joy that Ming spoke her mind. Masuyo was not expecting that response, her face was drained of what little colour she had, she avoided commenting.

'Where are Audra and Akanya?'

'Akanya asked for quiet time, and Audra, sadly is sedated and in the sanatorium, resting. Both will be back with the group tomorrow. I have taken you completely into my trust in this matter.'

Damn secrecy, that old horned-devil of destruction, Patience thought. She was over this charade and looked forward to working with real people in the real world of Pakistan.

They walked to the coffee shop, desperate for a quiet contemplative cuppa.

'American-o got her way, I'm not surprised! We are the manageable fools!' Patience laughed.

'I don't mind being in India, but can see the unfairness in how people are allocated. Akanya is a protected species in here.'

'Mexico, Pakistan, Timbuktu, wherever the work is, it's what we've committed to, that matters! The thing that bothers me is how injustice prevails in pursuit of justice.' Patience felt this annoyance grow with the irritation of a skin rash.

Ming whispered, 'I know.'

IN THAT FRENZIED STATE, Patience threw caution to the wind, she wrote a letter to Grace on how she felt, with the nagging doubt whether her sister would receive this somewhat scathing letter.

My dearest Grace,

Surprise! Another letter sooner than expected I'm sure!

I would have called you or arranged a chicken curry feast to calm my irritation, had I been at home. I can't wait to get out of this place! The training, I will maintain, has been good, the work I will do over the next three months is worthwhile, but will I sign up again for the same in here, I think not! I kid you not!

I have been allocated Pakistan as the place where I will serve for three months, and then homeward bound! Hallelujah! Apparently, I can call you once a month! I can't wait to hear your voice. So much yet to tell you. The people I've met, the situations I've encountered — that's a very long story that will be told over many cups of coffee, or perhaps a strong Irish beverage of choice when we meet. Can you hear me clear my throat? I miss you so much...

Until then, know I am safe, miffed, but safe my dear Grace. Love to you and your dashing man. Don't miss me too much. Patience xxx

28

A NEW WORLD ORDER

Felicity's trip to The Hague was not entirely a wasted one. What made this missing aircraft any different to the others that disappeared? She created awareness as the face of the truth she carried — not some news media item that could be switched off — forgotten — gone down in history — a cold case. Media attention escalated the matter when she made waves at The Hague.

MASUYO TURNED on the television in her private boudoir, a mother, and daughter escape from the world of the mission. Zuri lay next to her, coiled in a foetal position. The reporter's tense voice, a hard monotone, grabbed their attention as Singapore's Changi Airport sailed into view.

'It's been three months since the flight bound for an unknown location in Thailand, allegedly carrying a hundred-and-fifty women left on an unknown mission. None of the families and associates of these missing women have a clear knowledge of what the mission's purpose was, or its precise location. In an interview with Felicity Cassano, Australian legal correspondent on this matter, who is currently on a visit to The Hague, had this to say:

Felicity sat on a high stool dressed in a black sleeveless dress with a long string of pearls. She looked directly at the camera.

It's preposterous that something of this international magnitude is ignored. The question is, is this because the missing passengers are female, that it goes unnoticed, or without too much attention? How on earth does this happen, once again, in an age of sophisticated techno-logical detection? Families need answers! What are governments going to do to find these women and bring them home? Will The Hague issue a deadline on this?

Masuyo snapped off the television.

'The hype outside is growing, it's a good thing we plan to leave here soon.'

'Yes, mother, but does this put a damper on future missions here?'

'For a while, it will, until we are not perceived as a renegade group. Like all wars, this attention will die down, and we may move on with future missions.'

'Are we really, technically speaking, at war on global gender leadership?' Zuri's curiosity craved answers.

'My metaphorical use of 'war,' is that it has reached a height-ened state from 'hashtag metoo' through to extensive workplace harassment, mismanagement by heads of state and unjust socio-economic gender politics.'

'That was strategic mother, setting up the meeting with the field recruits for late tonight. It allows them to contemplate what the expectations of their roles are, once they get back to their quarters to retire for what's left of the night.' Zuri smiled in admi-ration, scanning her mother's often emotionless face for her reaction.

'You have indeed grown so wise, Zuri. I'm so proud of all you have learned and achieved. We know the strength of our gender, but the truth is when unhappy or facing new situations, we engage in a cross-section of unnecessary chatter which has the potential to mar passion and destroy relationships.'

Zuri listened, remembering the hours of contemplative solitude she was trained in, as a child. She knew through the experience of others, much older women; that much could be gained from silence, knowing when to strategically say what would benefit the greater good. She learned early on that a careless word, eroded great possibilities.

AT 8 PM that evening the ten field recruits who were invited to a meeting, sat in a smaller meeting room, waiting for Masuyo to arrive.

PATIENCE POPPED her letter to Grace in the outgoing box. She shook her head at the ridiculousness of labelling it the 'outgoing mail' box when there was no room for confusion with the absence of an 'incoming mail' box. A niggling doubt made her question if her letter would be proofread? She was cautious, played by the rules in her last two letters to Grace — she chose being compelled by the truth over being compliant, in this letter.

'TRUTH, Understanding, and Compassion sisters, thank you for being punctual to this late meeting,' Masuyo greeted.

Akanya and Audra were among the ten, sitting next to each other. The thing the mission got right, was making individuals agree to disagree, implying that diversity of thought was valuable. If they worked on the secrecy code with the same verve, this would make their overall ideology a godsend.

This way of thinking locked Patience in, as much as she

disagreed with some aspects of the mission's modus operandi — the gelling of people to a common purpose was close to Varuna's and Elsie's lessons, in her growing up years.

MASUYO WAS AN ADMIRABLE WOMAN, her own plight strengthened her unshakable resolve. She had uncanny insight into the souls of those she worked with, tapping into their fire to meet the mission's agenda. The swapping of countries was delivered with deft smoothness and respect that had the power to squash thoughts of further dissension.

She was dressed in a white tailored suit, black tie and stilettoes. A white beret sat at an angle on her loose hair. She harnessed male and female as she stood before the pairs of eyes that had never seen her gender fluidity before. She needed to depict this inner strength, outwardly in what she was calling the women to serve — the propelling of young women in leadership that went well beyond the twenty-first century.

She continued with humility and strength, the combination which was the basis of the mission's ideology.

'I am pleased to announce that the ten countries represented among us tonight will be well served. You have been placed as follows.' The screen behind her lit up with the names and photographs of each recruit, and the countries allocated.

A faint buzzing of voices passed through the room, then a quiet nod of acknowledgement of each recruit present.

'Some are still unsure if they will serve the three months, those negotiations are ongoing. You need not concern yourself with that, you have a bigger mission ahead of you. You will no longer be part of the whole group to allow for further intensive training and information in your preparation for the field.' She studied the faces in the room, keen to detect their unspoken thoughts.

'As some of you are aware, delegates from HQ are at your

locations now, to walk you through what you have to do. Your stamina is needed, the days and nights are long. You are on the brink of being a significant cog to a New World Order, shaping women as leaders of tomorrow, or some may be ripe for taking over now.' She smiled, looking for returned smiles. Receiving acknowledgement from others was high in her personal expectations.

'Military and parliamentarian training are part of the package. You carry the values instilled here and from your life outside. It is expected that you will visit schools, handpick new girls and spread the word of the mission. A New World Order is moving towards the horizon.

She straightened her back, pride, and determination beaming through her.

'Truth, Understanding and Compassion must be the platform from which you raise awareness, in preparing our women for the future.

Patience felt the change in Masuyo's tone, her voice grew louder, her jaw tightened as she stared ahead, looking through them in delivering her hypnotic message.

'Peace must reign in this world, we want an end to hostility among nations, families, religious sects. Violence must end — women and children suffer the most. Poverty must be history. Hunger, anger and aggression are destructive to our survival. It is in your hands now. Make a difference!'

Zuri's haloed look glowed with pride Her eyes were transfixed on her mother.

'No girl in the community you serve, should be illiterate, you will provide the tools for effective communication, both written and verbal, voice must be the power of our women — you will shape an intellectual and social force that cannot be matched, equal and above our male counterparts — we are creating 'Ladies as Leaders.' You will light the souls of the future against injustice.' She saw a raging fire within Zuri, love and compassion were evident in the inclining of her head, the lion and the lamb, melting the hearts of those mesmerised by the promise of her message.

ZURI TOOK control of the Q & A session.

'No question is too small nor unnecessary, please raise your questions now.'

Audra's hand rose, half-bent with trepidation, her voice quivered.

'What if the girls we select are resistant to a New World Order? What should we do?'

Masuyo's jaw stiffened, she looked up at Audra, her fiery eyes ablaze, her voice now soft and calm. Audra felt the hair on her neck curl. Zuri stepped aside to allow her mother to address the question.

'You would be discerning in your choice, you will know the soul with the potential for greatness. If not, then this mission has failed you.'

Not a sound was heard in the stillness created by that abrupt comment.

Akanya raised her hand, confident that she had a valuable question that needed an answer.

'Will the mission delegates be present at our stations throughout the three months we are there?'

'They will only be there to settle you in, they will then move off to other centres to begin the process for the next batch of new field recruits. This is a cyclical process.'

Akanya raised her hand again like a persistent student needing attention, wanting to be seen and heard.

'Will we have contact with our people, I mean families and communities we worked in before coming here?' Her grand circular gesture in her emphasis on 'families and communities' was shot down.

'Your question surprises me,' Masuyo planted a steady look in Akanya's direction, 'you are on a selfless mission, remember that.'

Uneasy silence followed the dismissal of Akanya's question. Masuyo's twitching jaw did not go unnoticed. Through clenched teeth, she added, 'you will be given a mobile telephone for official business. That is all I'm saying at this point.'

Akanya mumbled a hurried thank you, and sat down, wanting the earth to swallow her. She relived the fear of her childhood — chastisement and dismissal for her stupidity.

Patience cringed at the embarrassment Akanya felt, her maternal touch at the mission eased and aggravated many, she carried the shame and torment from her past, close to her skin, hidden in abundant, radiant smiles.

She pondered why the monthly telephone calls she was informed about, was not mentioned. She raised her hand to remove attention from Akanya.

'May we invite influencers to inspire those we serve, our charges, if I might call them that?'

'That can only be done with prior consent from HQ. My journey with you ends here when you depart to the field. I do envision seeing you again through the corridors of the New World.'

Tonight, there were no cheers, no applause, and no smiles.

'Please retire for the night, we shall reconvene tomorrow morning for a series of workshops that will run throughout the day to test your mettle. Come with five goals by morning, one personal and four you hope to achieve for the mission. Rest well, may Truth, Understanding and Compassion guide our elected goals.'

She stepped off the platform with her shoulders upright, looking straight ahead. The spotlight moved with her, Zuri sidled up to her mother, looping her arm through Masuyo's. They disappeared out the back door.

29

HOME IN AUSTRALIA

Felicity rushed back from The Hague to be with Alf, his health deteriorated while she was away. She cancelled her two day stopover in Sydney.

ANDREW LANG and Grace had breakfast together after a hectic ER evening. One patient was attended to under police guard which added a different stress dimension to their work night. The young man threatened people at Central Station ranting that he had a bomb in his bag. He was picked up by the police who received a call on the young man's crazed antics. He was disorientated, high on ice, the poison that was corrupting youth on the streets.

'It was tense last night, almost like a Hollywood movie,' Andrew said.

'Yeah, every threat to civilian safety has to be escalated as a priority. I'm glad he was removed before he caused any physical harm.'

'I have morbid dreams of ER being swamped by such a crisis.

How will we cope when we are short-staffed? I pray we never live to see this.'

'Dear God, yes! We cannot allow these dark thoughts to eat away at us, you know.'

'Any news on Felicity's husband, is he doing any better?'

'Nothing more since the last message and I really don't want to bombard her with questions about his health. She has a lot to deal with now, the question on what else transpired at The Hague, has to be put on hold. At least the situation has international attention, after her rumblings.'

'Hopefully, soon, there will be good news. I can't imagine what the waiting must be like for you.'

Grace's calm acceptance of the situation was only because she had proof that Patience was alive, writing letters to her, although sparse in detail, unlike her usual garrulous communication. But she was alive... that is all that mattered now.

'I've left that in God's hands now, I'm in a quandary about whether I should up and go to attend Keefe's mother's funeral. I feel awful to leave you carrying the can again. The funeral is scheduled for Friday week.'

'Don't be ridiculous, you promised me it was going to be family first in your life, Grace. What's changed? You have to go!'

'Mmmm... yeah I know, I should book a flight, I think, to get there early next week. Are you sure, you don't mind me leaving you again in a short space of time? I will think about it.'

'Think about it?' Andrew looked at Grace, confused by her vacillating attitude, 'I can't believe I'm hearing you say this. Please don't regret not going. I live everyday with not attending my mother's last rites because I let work get in the way. It's not worth the emotional baggage it will create, it cost me my relationship with my siblings.'

Grace trusted Andrew as her true friend, and advisor. They had come a long way together from his early infatuation with her, to his deep respect for what she stood for.

'That scares me, I've had that trauma with concealing my truth; I won't be able to live through another similar episode in my life. My mother went to her grave not knowing what troubled me for so many years.'

'Book that ticket, go for the week of the funeral, Keefe needs you there, he's too polite to ask you.'

'Thank you, Andrew. I needed to hear this, thank you, I will book my ticket today.'

Andrew reached across and squeezed her hand. There were days when he knew her like a book, and then on days like this he was left confused about her faltering indecision. She knew he was the second person to Patience who understood her, Keefe was learning every day.

She remembered Patience's words, 'every girl needs a good male friend, and lovers and husbands need to accept that fact of life if things are to remain sane between them.' Patience's outspoken views on women rang with truth and sensibility.

'Do you have much planned today, other than hitting the hay soon?'

'No, not really. Why, what are you thinking?'

'I need a beach walk, care to join me after breakfast?'

'I need the vitamin D, so yes count me in.'

'Vitamin D! Here I was thinking my dear friend would like to spend a few more hours with me.' Grace laughed, reaching out to playfully punch him on the arm.

'That too, I need more Grace-time. Keefe has the lion share now!' he teased.

They stepped out into a beautiful autumn morning, made for a beach walk after a strenuous night.

KEEFE CALLED AT AROUND 6 pm.

'Hello *mo ghrá*, how are you today after your night in ER?'

'The same old, you know how it goes. Felicity is back from The Hague, sooner than expected. Alf is in ICU and she needs to be with him.'

'Sorry to hear that. Will you go over to Melbourne to be with her then?'

'No, actually I arrive in Belfast on Tuesday morning to be with you when you lay mam to rest.'

Keefe was quiet on the other end, thinking how lucky he was to have found a supportive, caring and undemanding partner. He heard Grace's concern on the other end.

'You there Keefe? Hello?'

'Sorry... thank you for coming, you have no idea how happy I am to hear this.'

'You went silent on me, I thought perhaps you might not have wanted me there at this time.'

'Never, Grace, I know you have so much to attend to, that you have met mam is all I could have hoped for. I can't wait to see you.'

'Me too. Leave some of the funeral arrangements to me, I'll help Aileen with whatever still needs to be done.'

'To be honest, there's nothing to do, mam's parish members asked to be given the honour to arrange her last rites because she did so much to support them over the years. All I have to do is confirm the catering for the wake. Mam wanted it at the restaurant where she and dad hosted their wedding reception, back in the day. It became their favourite haunt.'

Grace had a lump in her throat hearing of the love they shared, and that mam cherished that to the end of her days.

Thoughts of her father's death returned, her mother was too distraught with his tragic, untimely passing to arrange anything. They had a small, quiet burial, which remained a blur in her memory. They returned home to a meal the neighbour cooked for them. The family pulled away, amidst vicious rumours about her father's death. Elsie helped them cope, with her quiet assistance, in running the home.

They chatted a bit about Patience. Keefe said he saw Felicity's interview on the news in Ireland. They parted happily that they would meet soon, albeit under sad circumstances.

THE NEXT MORNING Grace decided to attempt another beach walk. She needed her stamina to get things ready on the professional front, and to be ready to support Aileen and Keefe during their bereavement.

A gloomy morning sky, with autumn sunshine hidden under a blanket of heavy gathering clouds, threatened her intention. She had to make a dash to get in her walk. A hurried letterbox check revealed Patience's letter, hidden behind other mail.

Her heart raced, should she go back upstairs to read it, or walk first, and then stop to read it? She turned to return to her apartment, had second thoughts, quickened her pace and headed towards the beach. Patience's three month stint was coming to an end, perhaps this letter was that she was returning home soon. She stopped two streets down on the corner of Hodder Street and plonked herself down on the seat close to the bus stop.

She ripped open the envelope, two pages fell out, one handwritten, one typed. Her stomach looped a few times, she closed her eyes, fighting back the memory of Patience being held hostage in the chief's kraal in rural Natal. The short letters from Petros who risked his life to bring her home filled her thoughts — Patience was unreachable, there was no one to bring her home this time. She felt the first drop of rain hit the top of her head.

She picked up Patience's letter first, her heart sang, please, please, tell me you are coming back home. Drat! She kicked herself for not carrying her reading glasses. With the letter held at the furthest readable point, she screwed up her eyes to read her sister's letter. The words that caught her attention were, *I can't wait to get out of this place!* She froze, too afraid to read on. She peered at the letter again, her heart sank lower. Patience had committed to the additional three months in Pakistan. What possessed her to go on when she knew how stressed Grace would be.

She picked up the typed letter and read it. The letterhead had the words, 'The Mission' before the message which read,

Congratulations! Ms Patience Sharvin has been selected to represent the mission in Pakistan for three months in selecting and training young women for the future. She will be in touch once she has settled at the mission in Pakistan.

The letter was signed off, simply, *HQ,* followed by the slogan: *Propagating a New World Order.*

No name of the actual sender was included. The brief, formal letter made her edgy, the actual location in Pakistan was unnamed. The hard facts about the work Patience would engage in was left undisclosed. She called Andrew who promised to get to her soon. He told her to wait where she was.

How could Patience leave her in limbo? How irresponsible and how unlike her to do this! Virginia Bale was kind enough to look after things for her, surely she knew the urgency needed to return home. Anger and fear chipped at her thoughts, feeding her disappointment. Will she even know her sister as she remembered her? Had she been brainwashed? This mission seemed to be a cult. She had no control in this situation, all she could do was hope for the best.

The rain that threatened her morning, arrived in all its gushing glory, drenching her to the skin. She sat like an obedient, bedraggled puppy, waiting for Andrew.

He rushed up to her forlorn figure on the bench, swept her up in his arms, holding her close, whispering, 'we have to get you out of the rain.' She clung to him, afraid for herself as much as she was afraid for Patience. She was surprised when she heard

Andrew say, 'Oh hi Beth,' then she heard Beth Hobbs, her ER nurse say, 'Good morning Andrew, Dr Sharvin' and then hurried footsteps leaving. Grace pulled away from the crook of Andrew's neck.

'Oh dear God, can things get any worse this morning?'

'What do you mean?'

'That was Beth Hobbs, the grapevine queen in our facility! Can you imagine the news going around after she saw us together, in what might have appeared to be a compromising situation, to her anyway!'

'Who cares, Grace, let her set the grapevine alight! Show me the letters you received. May we go back to your place, this rain is not going to let up.'

ANDREW REREAD THE LETTER, confused by the mission letters, T U C, in bold typeface in a vertical arrangement below the supposed signature.

'This is a strange letter, what does 'New World Order' mean, is this some sort of take-over? You have to hand these letters to the investigating body in Canberra today. I'll make you some breakfast if you don't mind, and if it means driving down to Canberra after you make that call, so be it.'

Andrew's forthright approach was necessary.

30

AUSTRALIA AND IRELAND

Grace hit a roadblock, hope dwindled.

The letter from the mission led to silence from Canberra, with no new leads. She contacted the families and associates of the missing Australians — none of them had received the mission letter, nor a letter from the missing women in recent weeks.

Felicity called after Grace sent her a copy of the letters.

'She's covering up the real issue, she's not happy and we all know Patience is the easiest person in the world to please. The mission letter unnerves me the most, it says very little, yet so much is open to interpretation.'

'I feel the same way, do you think Patience is in physical danger? I worry that she might have been brainwashed in some way.'

Grace had to ask the question that disturbed her the most.

'No, not in any physical danger, I think, but her skills are being exploited. If she is entirely led by her heart, then I fear brainwashing is a real possibility. That is my seat of discontent. Compassionate people have often been led astray, but I know your sister is a strong, rational woman.'

Grace heard the fear in Felicity's words.

'My sister has always been a people pleaser — remember when she was held up by the irate husband in her apartment when his wife was moved to a safe house? Well, Patience was more concerned that the man would feel let-down because she tipped off the police.

'This is beyond that, we are dealing with an organisation, not a lone wolf, or a crazed husband. Who knows how many people she has to pander to?'

'Canberra's silence on the situation now, compared to the earlier concern and desire to find the passengers is disappointing. I'm inclined to think they might know more than they're letting on.'

'I got the uncanny feeling, in The Hague, people were reluctant to use their power to get involved, and yet this is an international crisis.'

'There's the promise of a telephone call which I live for, that's all we can do now. Pardon my rudeness in not asking after Alf. How is he doing?'

'He's back home now, I have a resident carer to assist me. I'm coping, I think. Nothing more I can do, really.'

Felicity's blunt tone shut off her pursuit on more details after Alf's health. She knew better not to probe — Felicity was so different to her, in so many ways, yet they both protected their private lives with fierce passion. Was it people who were bitten by life that became vigilant in shutting off others, either as anti-social individuals or unbearably pushy in their interactions?

Weakness became the enemy of two strong women when they were under fire from criticism. The only secret Patience ever revealed, years later, was her unspoken love for Petros Sibaya. His death under bizarre circumstances after he rescued her from the Chief's kraal, lived with Grace too.

'Look, I'll try to tap into my Canberra contacts for more leads.'

'Thank you, Felicity, you have enough on your hands now, so please, only if you can fit this in, don't neglect anything you have to do for Alf. He's your priority.'

AS THE DAYS ROLLED ON, news of the missing aircraft and its hundred-and-fifty female passengers disappeared from prime-time television and radio broadcasts.

GRACE ARRIVED, in Belfast on Tuesday, to a warm May morning. Keefe was unshaven, his creased shirt and crumply pants suggested he had been wearing them overnight. Sparse sprigs of red hair protruded from his chin and cheeks. He appeared thinner, his eyes were puffy and red. She dismissed the thought that he might be drowning in too many whiskey glasses. Reassurance flooded back when she inhaled the familiar spicy, woody perfume in his tight embrace. He whisked her off for breakfast.

He chose the private booth at the back of a casual, cosy cafe for solitude with Grace, away from the distractions of the world, and before the rush leading up to mam's funeral on Friday.

All Grace wanted was a cup of coffee, Keefe coerced her into having poached eggs and a shared choice of sausage. They sat huddled in the tight booth, Keefe reached across for her hands and held onto them.

'I missed you *mo ghrá,* thank you for coming.'

'Life is not the same when you're not around, that scares me. Andrew told me I had to be here for you, that I should not put work before you.'

'He's a good man, the most unselfish man I know. He is still smitten with you, anybody can see that — I have to be careful.'

He tried to smile but the heavy sadness in his eyes prevented it.

'How are you doing, Keefe?' Grace knew a direct question was necessary to get Keefe to open up, to shrug his stoic bravado — mam was everything in his world. He wanted her to live a perfect life after all her years of hardship in single-handedly raising him and Aileen.

'I'm getting there, one day at a time. It's a slow process accepting that I will never see her face again, nor hear her laughter and concern whenever I called her.'

'I'm glad I'm here.'

Keefe stared out the window as his coffee grew cold. Grace felt the brewing of something else embedded in his sadness.

'Is there anything else going on Keefe? You are not yourself, I know you are grieving, but there's something going on. I feel it.'

'Aye, *mo ghrá*, you know me so well.'

Slowly he released the tension eating at him. His ex-wife called to sympathise and invited herself to the funeral. She claimed that mam promised her a share of her possessions. Aileen was livid at the audacity of the claim, knowing full well that mam was unhappy in his choice of a wife. Now a letter arrived from his ex-wife's solicitor demanding disclosure of the will before the funeral. Keefe sighed, saddened by this horrible turn of events to what was to be a peaceful farewell, to his beloved mam.

'Mam was a simple woman. She had nothing except what Aileen and I provided in her later years. She protested whenever we indulged her a little, calling us wasteful, saying the poor needed the things we gave her, more than she did.'

'What an amazing woman, I'm reminded of my old neighbour, Mrs Beresford, who lived for her children, much like my own mother, but sadly Mrs Beresford's daughter did not return her mother's, unconditional love. Mam was blessed with two devoted children and that was all she needed.'

Keefe managed a faint smile, needing to hear Grace's soothing acknowledgement of the love he shared with his mam.

'We had to engage a solicitor to handle this sudden claim, but it seems we have to attend a disclosure of the will on Thursday morning.' His eyes reddened, 'how can I do this the day before I put mam to rest, *how*? I pleaded for an extension until after the burial. It was declined.'

'I'm so sorry to hear this. It puts a lot of pressure on you and Aileen.'

'Aye, we don't need this now. How do you feel about meeting my ex-wife at the funeral, she will be in your face if I know her. I should have told you this before you got here.'

'Don't you worry about me now, I will be just fine. I am here for you, and Aileen, nothing else matters.' She concealed her anxiety, avoiding Keefe's pleading look.'

THAT EVENING after dinner at Aileen's apartment, both women sat down to chat as Keefe nodded off on the couch.

'He's exhausted, Grace. This situation with Siobhan has left him blaming himself for her interference in his life and mine. To be honest, we should have seen this coming.'

Grace felt the gloom since her arrival, had elevated, leaving her not quite sure what to say. She feared her presence in Keefe's life might have contributed to the problem.

'Do you think she knows about our engagement?'

'Oh, aye, she knows every move he makes, her cronies are everywhere, minding our business. Bunch of blasted nasties, I tell you! Sorry, Grace, I'm so upset with her for insisting we do this before the funeral. How insensitive, but then again, that is why the marriage crumbled. We offered her anything she wanted but begged to let us send mam off in peace. She's been crying poverty to mam for many years, so I won't be surprised if mam did indeed promise her something. Where's her decency to wait while we are in mourning.'

Aileen was just as distracted as Keefe. She needed to vent her pent-up emotions. She held back the tears, feeling comfortable opening her heart and frustrations to Grace.

'Mam, God bless her, gave Siobhan money whenever she could, although Keefe gave her a handsome divorce settlement. That was the most costly, short-lived marriage I know.'

'Why does she cry poverty. They have no children so what is it?'

'Truth be told, she's an inveterate gambler, bleeding everyone to feed her addiction. It's just awful.'

Grace didn't comment, struggling to reconcile how someone like Keefe married someone like Siobhan.

'I hope this ends once she knows if she was left anything.'

'Who knows, we won't look at the will until we are forced to, it makes my heart bleed, that even in death, an outsider wants to steal the dignity from mam's send-off. I'm sure you haven't experienced this in your family.'

'Both my parents have passed on, there was no such thing. My sister and I valued our mother's love and their time with us was enough, not to care about anything else. But, I do know of others who turn bestial during this time of grieving.'

'You and your sister are decent folks, not gamblers and people scavenging money off unsuspecting people. I appreciate being able to talk to you about this. It makes Keefe stressed when I rant and rave over the situation.'

Keefe opened his eyes, embarrassed that he had nodded off. His coy smile, like that of a little boy who had fallen asleep over his dinner, melted Grace's heart.

Aileen invited them to stay over that night, Keefe was pleased that Grace accepted. Seeing them both bond lightened his grief and stress for what else would emerge in the days leading up to man's funeral.

~

ON THURSDAY MORNING, the reading of mam's will was held at the local court house, Aileen sobbed throughout the proceedings — there was no promise of, nor a request to hand over any of mam's humble possessions to Siobhan. On the contrary, most was left to mam's church, much to Aileen's and Keefe's relief.

A beautiful service was held on that sunny Friday morning, befitting mam's selfless life.

On Sunday afternoon, Keefe, Grace, and Aileen flew to Australia to help Grace piece together the puzzle to Patience's whereabouts. Aileen needed a break away from the family noise in Belfast.

31

DEPARTURE TO THE FIELD

At 11 pm on the night of departure, Masuyo met with the field recruits. She was in a black kimono, her hair was pulled tightly to the centre of her head, giving her an austere, stretched forehead. She had a grave message to issue to those heading out to the field.

With an unflinching serious visage, she outlined that some peace keepers had private agendas that put young women and girls at greater peril, with human trafficking and horrific corruption in the name of social justice.

She stressed that their location had to remain undisclosed, to prevent detection, and a disruption to the mission's work. She added that for this reason, all devices such as phones, cameras and lap-tops had to be confiscated. When questioned on why this was not made transparent before the women signed up, Masuyo said, nobody would have wanted to sign up, as this measure implied they were being held against their will, which is not the mission intention. She spoke of trust in the modern world.

'We live in an era where trust is inclined to have many shades of meaning, its bent and twisted to suit the agendas of the most despicable individuals. Altruism is misrepresented and social justice is slandered. Our mission has to operate as an underground movement if we are to survive and change the world as we envision it. The word 'mother' which is so dear to us all — regardless of what we have faced in life, brings the nurturing and compassion that is needed to lead us into a new world. Truth and understanding remove all forms of negative human patterns of behaviour. Slave trade, sex trade, children being kidnapped for illegal international adoption rings have to be stopped. We have to do this together.'

Patience knew that this idealistic notion, while noble, was either never going to create that nirvana, although a halfway measure might be possible. Cynicism was never her way, reason made her see the possibilities. She was committing to the new world with every fibre of her being, halfway there was better than not moving forward at all.

Masuyo stood to attention, making her appear taller, legs apart, right hand in a fist raised up above her shoulders — she was a rebellious sight, different to the faces she presented in the last three months. She was militant, determined and ready for a new era. She yelled, microphone free, in a voice that reverberated up to the high-ceilinged roof.

She tapped her head with two fingers saying,

'Repeat, Truth!'

She touched her forehead with an open palm saying,

'Repeat, Understanding!'

She thumped her chest with her right hand, saying,

'Repeat, Compassion!'

This went on for three mantra rounds. Her final cry was.

'Go in Peace! Serve our women well!'

A staggered departure was arranged, pairing some, while others were set to leave alone, depending on the location of their allocated countries.

Ming and Patience were set to leave the mission together —

India and Pakistan being territorially close, meant they might be on the same flight out.

Patience heard the familiar hovering sound of a helicopter, at close proximity, just as she had heard, the night before Alva was sent back to her family.

She slapped her chest saying, 'Repeat, Compassion!' psyching herself for what was ahead.

I⊤ WAS as black as hell, not a light, nor a star was in sight. A roped stairway and waist-buckled belts were thrown down from the hovering helicopter. Mouth guards were pulled across the lower half of their faces, mouths and noses were covered, goggles were strapped across their eyes, and ear muffs were stuffed in place. All they were told to do was look skywards.

As they ascended the rope, with Ming ahead of Patience, an uncanny thought crossed her mind — was she literally underground these past three months? She risked a backward, downwards glance — there was nothing but a vast black void.

Ming froze midway on the way up. Patience's calf muscles ached, the sedentary lifestyle she chose inside the mission, avoiding the state of the art gym and swimming pool was taking its toll. She heard a woman's voice on the loud hailer call out from the open door above them.

'Let yourself go, you are buckled in. Let go, I'll pull you in!'

'Do it, Ming, you won't fall, you will be pulled up.' Patience called out from behind her, the noise of the shuddering helicopter drowned her voice.

Patience felt her legs turn to jelly when Ming fell, dangling mid-air, like a rag doll. She had fainted... losing all sense of fear. She was flipped up with ease and pulled into the cabin. Patience was pulled by the arms, and flopped beside Ming.

PATIENCE WOKE to sun streaming on her face. She opened her eyes, blinked from the sharp, sheer blue of the sky she had not seen for many months. She shut her eyes again whispering, 'we are safe Ming. We are safe.'

She peered at the vacant seat beside her. She screwed up her eyes to get a glimpse of where she was.

She was on a rooftop overlooking a city skyline.

Ming was gone.

The pilot nodded and escorted her to the car at the entrance of the building. No words were spoken. Just nods and gestures. The pilot looked Japanese, the woman in the car outside the building was blonde. She wore heavily shaded sunglasses.

Patience was confused, wanting to ask if Ming was safe, she knew she would not get an answer. The mission was tight-lipped, never overtly lying to conceal the truth, but silent.

Arriving at the airport came with the shocking realisation that she was in Western Australia. Was she in Perth all this time, so close to home, so close to Grace? She had no idea how she got to the rooftop landing pad. Her body ached, she felt dizzy, needing a painkiller to soothe her aching, heavy head.

Patience left Perth that afternoon with the blonde-haired woman on a flight to Karachi.

THE MISSION STATION in Pakistan was in a remote location where young women and girls were secretly educated and prepared to lead the vision for a New World Order.

Patience's room was basic, a single rickety bed with a thin blanket. A set of clothes lay on the bed, a long dress, and pants and a headscarf. She was to be in disguise in traditional clothes. Her room was in a family home. The Akbar family had three teenage daughters and a two-month-old baby boy. They received Patience with warmth, yet beneath the surface, fear lurked.

Akbar was a wheat farmer, an educated man whose daughters could read and write. He built an underground classroom beneath the wheat fields, under an abandoned, unused well.

Patience's mission assistant who had remained silent throughout the journey was placed with another family to avoid detection.

It was 9 am Sydney time when Grace heard her mobile phone ringing in the distance. She struggled to open her heavy-lidded eyes after getting off shift that morning. It was a hectic and emotional week in Belfast, and she went back to work that Friday night. She collapsed in an exhausted heap after her shift, dead to the world until her phone taunted her into a wakeful state. She stretched for her phone on the bedside table. Keefe purred like a giant cat beside her, undisturbed by her ringing phone. His belligerent ex-wife's antics in the week of mam's passing had left him a drained wreck.

With an unsteady hand, Grace croaked into her phone,
'Hello, Grace speaking.'
There was a moment's silence.
'Grace! Oh, how lovely to hear your voice, even when it's a croak! Were you asleep *girrrl*?' Patience laughed.
Grace sat up in bed, unable to say anything, she cleared her throat, jumped out of bed, walking around like an emergency was on hand.
'Patience, I don't believe it! Where are you?'
Part of her hoped that she would hear that Patience was at the airport waiting to be picked up.
'I'm in Pakistan! On a mission assignment, remember I said, in my letter, that I might be staying on for another three months.'
Grace's dry mouth made it difficult for her to respond. Patience's vibrant joy was unmistakable, and here she was utterly

disappointed that her sister had taken up the additional three months. All her fears that her sister might have cracked, or sunk into depression during her time away, were allayed now, yet she was disappointed that Patience did not sob, did not say she missed her. The light, the excitement in her voice was unchanged. In the distance, a space she tried to imagine, she heard Patience speaking to someone in the background.

'The line appears to have cut off... hello Grace... are you there... can you hear me... Grace?'

Grace jolted back to reality.

'I'm here, I'm here, I'm sorry, I'm in a daze as you can imagine. Are you well Patience, are you staying in proper accommodation? I've heard and read so many things about safety issues there?'

Patience's silence made her realise the call might be tapped, she should not be asking her sister questions that might well compromise her safety. Patience knew how to take care of herself, even if she was living under strenuous conditions.

'What's been happening while I've been away? Are you well, Grace?'

'I'm well, if you are. I'm counting the days to your return. I have so much to tell you. Don't stay any longer after this is over, please.'

'Hey, you *are* the sentimental one, I love being loved by you, sis! I promise I will be home after this term is over. I have to get back to assist Virginia.'

'You will be blown away with the work she's been doing and the love and care she gives Sprite and Ajax.'

'That's so good to hear. I miss my doggies! I abandoned them like a cruel mother. I'm eager to return to you, sis, you know that, right?'

'I can't wait to hear about your adventures.'

'Mmmm... not quite that, but many late nights of catching up for sure. What's new on your end with your besotted men,

Andrew, and Keefe? If I should be so lucky!' Her husky laugh made Grace smile.

'Oh, stop that, Andrew is a dear friend, you know that! The news is that Keefe and I got engaged in Belfast last month, just before his mother passed away.'

The line crackled and was dead.

Grace was devastated that Patience was cut off before she could respond to her crucial news. She craved confirmation that Patience approved, was happy for her, she needed to hear it from her.

The waiting began once again...

32

ON THE FIELD

Culture and language connect the world when a desire to understand dominates.

Patience had the ability to embrace culture and traditions with ease. It was never good enough to just know people, she had to explore what made those around her tick. Their dreams, visions and culinary delights intrigued her. Here in Pakistan, she craved to know more, it burned as her lifeblood.

Akbar treated as his eldest daughter, with enough respect that she was an older woman. He acted as a fatherly guide to ensure she understood the dynamics of the people and politics in her new environment.

Her safety was paramount to him. He stressed cautiousness whether she was at the Well Study Centre, or in the city on assignment to enlist young women into the mission training program. They spent many hours, late at night, in discourse about the gender divide, locally and globally. Having three daughters, made this his vested interest in supporting the mission's values. He gave up his teaching at the university in Lahore and bought the wheat farm as a place where he could fulfil his work with the mission, without drawing too much attention to himself. Young women who were enlisted in the training arrived as 'employees,' field hands and domestic staff to avoid suspicion and detection.

The question she had, that her fear and curiosity would not quell, was about the teacher who was responsible for the academic side of the young women's training. He was aloof, avoiding her with his downcast eyes and brief nod. This troubled her. They were expected to spend most of their day at the Well Study Centre.

'Who is the teacher at the centre? I know nothing about him and daresay he will never let me know. I think he's not happy with my presence. Tell me something about him to help me understand before the students arrive next week.'

'Azmil is a reliable, honest man, I assure you.' Akbar looked searchingly at Patience, feeling her unease, wanting her to believe she had nothing to fear.

'He never speaks, is it because English is the barrier between us? All I get is a slight nod, no eye contact at all.'

'He speaks the Queen's English, I assure you, my dear Patience, give him some time, he is a brilliant man. He's written a few books on women in a shackled world. His life circumstances made him reclusive, mistrustful of new people. He will thaw soon, I assure you.'

Patience felt uncomfortable with Akbar's crutch phrase, 'I assure you.' His deep enunciation of the hard 'r' sound when he spoke of Azmil made her doubtful. She had to make a conscious effort to note if this was his general crutch phrase or something he used as a cover up. Life had taught her to listen to the subtle nuances of language, and to that which was left unsaid, to help her understand new people and new encounters.

She was determined to get to know the tall, striking, aquamarine-eyed Azmil, with his lush head of dark, shiny hair and pale, almost transparent, complexion. He barely left the Well Centre.

Akbar did not tell her much, leaving her wondering about the mysterious, dashing Azmil.

A week after Patience's arrival at Akbar's abode, the first group of ten young 'employees' arrived on foot under the protection of two older women. Later she learned that the women escorting the young recruits were part of the mission. She recalled Masuyo saying that she would be expected to scout out girls for training before she left Pakistan. No conversation was exchanged with the women who brought the students to Akbar. They stayed the night and left before dawn, needing the protection of darkness.

Akbar's eldest daughter welcomed and introduced her to the new students, a group of curious-eyed young women. She spoke to them in Urdu and repeated the greeting in English. The young women ranged in age from sixteen to twenty.

Despite the long walk of many days, in the cold, bitter winter nights, they appeared eager. Chapped lips and cracked cheeks were attended to by Akbar's wife — she too, was a silent worker, smiling, nodding, saying nothing.

Patience got to the Well Centre at 9 am that morning with Akbar. The centre was beneath an abandoned well in a corner of the wheat field. Akbar threw a stone onto the concrete lid below. After three repetitive stones hit the bottom, the lid lifted, then a mechanised steel ladder rose with swift ease to the top of the well, inviting Akbar's and Patience's entry. Akbar said something in Urdu, all Patience understood was 'Azmil.'

When they got down to the bottom of the well, and into the underground entrance, the exposed steel ladder retracted and the door slammed shut above them. Azmil greeted Akbar with his hand over his heart, his head lowered, and went back to his class-room. He had the young women, standing up on their chairs reciting Maya Angelou's 'Still I Rise.'

Akbar smiled at Patience, 'Queen's English right, and a brilliant poem, what a combination!'

Somehow Patience felt more relaxed. Her fascination with wanting to know more about Azmil grew in that moment. She would reach out to him to make him comfortable around her. He was outrageously good-looking, she wondered how the girls avoided being distracted by his mesmerising aquamarine eyes. She could almost hear Grace's voice in her head, 'keep on task sis, no distractions, not here!'

Akbar left to continue with his work for the day, checking on workers, communicating with the mission and writing his book, titled quite simply, 'Girls' Education in Pakistan.' He was living just beneath the radar of obliteration. This was a violent country, openly provoking change on gender expectations for women, invited a death warrant.

The first day with students at the Well Centre was an enjoyable one. She overheard part of Azmil's lesson, 'I will expose you to literature that will bring the world to you, right here. It will make you want to soar to make a difference. Reading, and education will remove you from the slums of life.'

The young women were excited when Patience came into their classroom to speak to them. She returned the chorused greeting of *Assalamu Alaikum*, with *Mualaikumsalam* which Akbar told her was a permissible shortened version of returning a greeting. One of the young girls raised her hand, beaming from ear to ear.

'Akbar sir's daughter told us you were from Australia, tell us about your ancestry.'

She knew that new students were not to be given too much information on their backgrounds, she ignored that rule and proceeded.

'I am a naturalised Australian, I was born in South Africa, into a Zulu tribe, although I grew up outside the tribe with another family. My upbringing was different from what others from my birth tribe might have had. I am very grateful that I had two amazing mothers to guide me through life.'

The young women stared at Patience, their bright-eyed attention melted her heart.

'So, you are a bit like us, you know we are from the orphanage. We are not even sure if our parents died during the attack when we were separated, or whether we have been led to believe they were killed? You are so lucky to have two mothers, we don't even have one now.' The young woman spoke without emotion.

Patience patted her on the shoulder. She knew passions ran deep on the political front here, she had to keep her head and heart on her mission objective, to train women to become leaders with the versatility to lead anywhere in the world. In her first session she shared the values Varuna and Elsie instilled in her. The young women hung onto every word of the anecdotes she shared. She was breaking them in, sussing out their strengths — the communicators, the compassionate, the intellectual, and the silent ones, brutalised into silence from past traumas.

There was a mixed-bag of talents to work with, each a strength in its own right. These strengths had to be drawn out before she could bring new skills to them.

She realised Azmil was standing at the door of the classroom, unsure whether he was eavesdropping as she did on his lesson, she invited him in.

He looked at her with his aquamarine eyes for the first time. His expression was grave, his puckered brow made her fearful.

'*Assalamu Alaikum* Ms Patience,' he said in a soft voice. She returned his greeting, '*Mualaikumsalam* Azmil sir.'

She heard the young women refer to Akbar as 'Akbar sir.'

'No, please not 'sir', Azmil is enough. You and the young women cannot leave, just yet.'

Patience's heart skipped a beat, what did he mean? She looked at him, with a million questions darting in her head.

'Don't worry, I picked up a signal, a raid is on in the next village, which means the rebels will come snooping around here. We have to remain still, very still until they leave.'

'How do we do that? How do we tell the young women about this?' Patience felt her forehead moisten, she knew enough about violence in these parts to catapult her adrenalin. She had to remain calm.

'The young women are used to this, it is you I'm worried about. This is new to you.' He held his right hand over his heart as he spoke. There was a humble piousness about him.

'We will move further in, away from the entrance.'

'What about food? The students would be having dinner in an hour, Akbar sir will be worried if we don't return.'

'Don't worry. You have a kind maternal spirit, sister. I have canned food, it's just that we cannot warm the food, it will alert the nostrils of those greedy rebels.' He smiled through red, tea-stained teeth which made him appear much older than his beautiful face.

'Akbar will be aware that we had to stall the return of the students to the house.' His soft voice, with a light accent was soothing to the ear.

'Let's move the students then,' Patience felt the urgency of Azmil's message. More than anything it was the students they had to protect.

AN HOUR LATER, they heard gunshots, horses galloping overhead and muffled voices. They sat still, some of the young women were praying as gunshots continued to echo into the night. After a few hours the sounds of the horses' gallops faded into the distance, then absolute silence.

Azmil told them not to leave, rebels might well be lurking

around. Akbar would give them the all clear in the morning. A cold dinner of shared canned beans and corn was eaten, the young women were told to rest. Azmil gave them all the blankets and coats he had to keep them warm.

Seeing how he lived, made Patience understand why he was so lean, of pale complexion and reclusive. She had to wait out the night with him until Akbar arrived.

She did not expect to hear what Azmil spoke of that night.

It was well past 2 am when Azmil asked Patience about her life, and why she was on assignment with the mission. She told him everything from her abduction in South Africa through to her setting up of the Sisters Helping Sisters Organisation. She knew for him to trust her, he would have to understand who she is. He listened, staring at her during her recount of the time she was in the chief's compound, up to Petros' murder.

'You have brushed with death too. You have experienced life. You had the most wonderful mothers. The scriptures teach that 'Your heaven lies under the feet of your mother' — you embrace that, sister.'

Patience knew that a profound respect was beginning to develop between them. Almost without warning he confessed.

'I am a child born out of wedlock.'

Patience sucked in her breath, afraid to look up at him, knowing that would have been the most difficult thing for him to admit to a stranger.

He picked his head up slowly and looked at her.

'That is why I have committed myself to the mission. My mother was a young, beautiful, intelligent woman. An American delegate at the Peshawar Air Station fell in love her — it was mutual, I'm told. My grandmother knew my mother was pregnant and hid her away for nine months. When I was born, looking as I do, a neighbour reported the matter to a rebel leader who had my father killed. One day, eighteen months after I was born, my mother was outside the house, when rebels seized her, and we assume, killed her because we never heard of her again. I have no memory of her.' Patience felt her eyes sting and her ears burned as she listened to a story that made her own life traumas seem uneventful.

'Did your grandparents raise you?'

'My grandmother did until I had to be moved to the orphanage at the age of three when she passed away. Akbar heard of the situation and came to the orphanage one day, and took me home with him. I have been raised as his son. He wanted to send me to Australia or England to study, but, I refused. This is my birthplace, I want to serve my people. I studied at the university where he worked.' He paused. After five interminable minutes of awkward silence, he said, again, staring at the floor.

'I sunk into a depressive state, in my mid-thirties and gave up teaching at the university, and joined Akbar on this mission. I do this to honour my mother, she knew love. It was taken from her, my father loved her, but their lives together were not meant to be.

Patience listened to a life that had so much to offer, a life that could have been destroyed, had it not been for Akbar's noble act.

That night, two souls, locked in friendship, in their service to shaping the lives of women leaders of tomorrow, in a place where human life was disposable.

33

CONTEMPLATION

Patience sat under the bright quarter of the moon, swinging gently on the seat in Akbar's verandah. The tops of the wheat stalks swayed, brushing against each other in a ceremonial moonlit dance. Thoughts of Azmil's life circumstances consumed her. He could have chosen the dark path; joining rebel forces, instead, he dedicated his life to serving young women in gaining recognition, through their contributions to society. For all his early life struggles, he wanted to be a significant part of a society that had brutally taken his parents.

He yearned to be included as a man of worth, not one born out of wedlock, the bastard in his mother's American love affair. She saw herself in him, a kindred spirit as she, too, yearned for her cultural roots. It was an undeniable part of her. She was infused with a warm glow in recalling his mark of respect for the young, free-spirited mother that he never got to know.

Akbar watched her lost in thought, he was happy to see a faint smile on her lips. He hesitated at first, not wanting to disturb her contemplative solitude.

'Sister Patience, you should come in, it's quite chilly out here.

You had a big day and a big night, that you did not anticipate, and one I did not fully prepare you for. My intention was not to create fear.'

'Yes, it certainly was my baptism by fire, I'm not too cold, thanks. Please tell me more about Azmil. He is a fascinating person. He told me a bit about his birth and his mother and father, just a scattering of thoughts.'

'I'm surprised he let you into his world so soon. He sees into your soul, sister.'

'He told me you took him out of the orphanage and gave him a family and an education. Who could ask for more? You are a good man Akbar. I would have loved to have a brother like you. Azmil is indeed fortunate you took him in.'

'It would be an honour to be considered your brother, although I feel more like a father to you. You have this wonderful spirit where the child within shines through, drawing you to people.'

'Look the moon is hiding now, with all this praise going around,' she laughed. Tell me more about Azmil's fascinating history.'

'I heard of him through friends who lived in the neighbourhood close to his grandmother. To be honest, to this day, I do not know how the rebels left his grandmother untouched. God acts in mysterious ways, you know. As a widow, her survival, after her daughter's situation, was very bleak indeed.'

'He said a beautiful thing, that he was happy his mother died having known true love, not an iota of hatred nor unhappiness, what a pure thought.'

'He went through some dark days while studying and teaching at the university, as he might well have told you, which pushed me too in the mission's direction, to ensure our women are given a chance to be the best versions of themselves.'

'What are your plans for your daughters, Akbar?'

'I want them to study in Britain or Australia until the New World Order is in step. I don't want them to spend their adult years in Pakistan. My wife is concerned about this, but my plan is to get them all over to Britain or Australia, while I continue with more mission work here, until such time, when Azmil and I can join them.'

'Yes, I do understand why you would want this for your family.'

Akbar's wife came to the door with a blanket for Patience, motioning them to come indoors where she had a hot pot of tea and freshly fried samosas.

Patience looked at her serene face, she accepted Patience and the students with quiet, selfless warmth. The spirit of a mother was indomitable, no matter where one was in the world.

Pondering on her own life became a late-night ritual. The stillness of cold nights sent her mind off on a meander through her past, like a magic carpet hovering over visions of her younger self.

The resilience of this community, who continued to hang onto their dreams, even though they were under constant threat from militant forces, made her converse with her soul. Important aspects of life — freedom to love and pursue one's dreams, travelling to distant destinations, immersing one's self in different cultures and people, never before encountered. She saw selfless giving when one's own safety was at risk. She was captivated by this pure spirit.

Akbar was a man who led by example, rich in culture and spirituality, but moving with contemporary thinking on morality, gender and freedom to pursue dreams. Both Akbar and Azmil lived the words of their faith in their treatment and advancement of women. If a mother was respected, so too should the future mothers of the world be respected. They supported that you cannot venerate one and denigrate the other.

The memory of Varuna and Elsie came to mind on what they meant to her and Grace as formidable women, one vocal, the other placid. There was a universal resonance to how mothers were perceived.

GRACE WAITED in silent strength for the next telephone call from Patience. Another month came and passed — no call. Aileen spent three weeks in Sydney helping Grace gain some perspective on her sister's situation. She urged Grace to make a trip to Pakistan to set her mind at ease, in knowing that Patience was indeed there. Grace disagreed with the suggestion, knowing full well, that Patience would be unhappy with such interference, which suggested she was not responsible for her own safety.

'I don't understand,' Aileen said, 'won't she be happy to see you, and know that you love and care so much for her?'

Grace had to choose her words wisely.

'It's not that, her passion for serving others takes precedence in her world, she is headstrong and retreats when she suspects inference in her life.'

Grace knew that Felicity's interference in both their lives, irked Patience, but for the sake of friendship she often took it with a pinch of salt. She would incur Patience's anger if she turned up unannounced in this situation. Grace was grateful for Aileen's support in recent weeks with Keefe's increasingly long hours at work. She put it down to his paying back for the hours he took during mam's illness and funeral.

Later that afternoon Andrew called Grace to alert her to a Current Affairs screening that evening. Three women were being interviewed on their return home after the aircraft they were travelling in, had mysteriously deviated off the intended flight path.

Grace felt her heart sink to the floor. She broke out in a cold sweat as her anxiety took hold. She couldn't find the remote control to turn on the television, she coughed as her breath came in short asthmatic bursts. She stood in the middle of the lounge room dazed, when suddenly she realised the remote control was staring up at her from the coffee table. In her dash to grab it, she fell onto the couch in wanting to catch every bit of the interview.

Tonight's special segment is an interview with three of the passengers that were on board the flight that disappeared after it left Singapore, with no plausible answers to date.

The sullen, yellowy-pale faces of the women, one younger and two older, appeared in the background on the screen in the Current Affairs studio. Dull lifeless eyes stared straight ahead.

The women were introduced by their first names and countries, Alva from Sweden, Gertrude from Germany and Petra from Canada.

Gertrude spoke of her experience.

'It was not a place of torture, it was luxurious in many ways, but artificial, no sky, no sunlight, it was like being buried away in some forgotten city.'

The interviewer intervened.

'Do you think you were underground throughout the time you were there? Where was the aircraft during this time?'

'We arrived at the destination in the thick of night, we disembarked through a cavernous entrance, then down a long flight of wrought-iron stairs into the building. It did feel like it was deep below, somewhere. We never saw the aeroplane again.'

Petra appeared distant, her soft voice, hesitant, afraid in her Valium-induced communication. She said she felt spiritually enlightened by the mission's TUC philosophy and that the secluded lifestyle was healing for her. The interviewer did not pursue further questions with her.

Alva said she left earlier, due to illness. The interviewer probed for more information on how Alva left the mission.

'I was carried piggy-back onto a helicopter, and all I

remember is getting out of a van at the airport. I must have fallen asleep. I don't recall how I got there.'

Grace stared at the screen in disbelief, she called Keefe. He didn't pick up her call. She called Andrew, collapsing in a heap of tears when he arrived an hour later.

'I feel awful asking you to watch that interview. I had no idea we were going to hear what we did.'

'I'm glad I watched it, I have clarity now on what Patience is mixed up in. She was circumspect in what she divulged.'

'Don't judge her too harshly, she probably felt safe and did not want to distress you. As the German woman said, the place was luxurious.'

'What about mental health issues from being castigated this way, after the promise of so much that would have encouraged all these women to sign up?'

'Let me get you some of your calming South African tea, where is it Grace?' He walked into her kitchen like a devoted husband.

'The Rooibos tea is in the cupboard above the fridge, thank you, Andrew.'

'Have you called Keefe, again? Are you going to let his sister know? She has been very supportive, from what you've been telling me.'

'Not until I talk to Keefe. He's not picking up my calls, I'll wait until he gets home. I'm still reeling from the possibility that the passengers might have been at some underground location that nobody knows about.'

'Yes, this is a mystery, but there was no intention to harm the passengers if they were sent home as they wished.'

'Patience gave no indication where she was in her letters and they were post-marked, 'Singapore,' so they must have been in some location there.' Grace tossed this over and over again, willing her mind to believe that her sister was still in Singapore.

'I can't see how, Grace. Remember we heard that the flight left Singapore - that rules out that possibility.'

'I'm trying to remain optimistic, but everyday there's some new piece of the puzzle that does not fit. I don't know how involved my sister is in all of this. It must be a massive covert organisation.'

Andrew looked at Grace, seeing the stress she was under, for the second time in her life, he had to keep her in the moment.

'Here sip on this tea, and try calling Keefe again.'

'To be honest Andrew, he has been so preoccupied with his erratic hours since we got back from his mother's funeral. I don't know whether I should burden him with this now.'

'He will want to know, toss those silly thoughts now.'

Andrew heated dinner for her, tidied up and left her to wait for Keefe. She needed time alone with him to fill him in on the latest bit of news. Andrew was perfect in her imperfect world, she watched him leave, filled with sadness.

KEEFE ARRIVED AN HOUR LATER, his breath laced with the stench of whiskey.

'Is something the matter *mo ghrá*, I saw a few missed calls from you, I could not call back.' His eyes danced in pockets of fluid, and he could barely keep his head up. She hated hearing the slur at the end of his words. What happened to the debonair man she met in Amsterdam? It was unfathomable how he drove home in that inebriated condition, undetected by police.

'That's okay Keefe, we can chat in the morning. You need to hit the hay, so you go on. I'll be in soon.'

She watched him saunter to the bedroom, his unsteady gait obvious from one who had downed far too much alcohol, in a short space of time, drowning what he would not talk about.

She curled up in her favourite couch, letting the soft velvety folds envelope her.

Loneliness crept back into her life.

She wished Andrew had stayed a while longer, she wished Patience was there with her usual pragmatic advice.

The television played softly in the background, she stared up at the ceiling — she had to fight this battle on her own.

34

HOME

Patience made her first car trip, with Akbar's driver, to Karachi, to identify and recommend the next group of young women to be taken into the mission fold. Akbar warned her to proceed with caution.

Her contact at the orphanage was a man of middle years. Balthazar worked as an undercover agent for the mission. He was lauded as a man with a great vision on the future of women, both within and outside the country. He was a slight man, in a white, soft cotton suit. A black and white bandana framed his bony face.

She did not expect to be overcome by uncontrollable emotion when she saw babies in cribs and toddlers barely able to walk... their parents had been taken by the surge of violence that swept the country at any time. Floods of tears forced her to step outside for a while. Human cruelty was difficult to face in the flesh. She saw the struggles of the women at the Sisters Helping Sisters Organisation, but seeing children in arms, at the most pivotal stage of their lives, left abandoned, orphaned by inhumanity, tore her heart apart.

She spent the day at the orphanage and surrounding schools, scouting out the potential of future leaders, her heart wanted to take them all, sweep them into her arms and love them like she was loved in her brilliant childhood.

She was at the orphanage under the guise of being a prospective parent. Some of the older girls swarmed around her, clambering for her attention, others watched her from a distance with suspicion loaded in their eyes.

Balthazar provided a list of names he had singled out for the girls he recommended she should shadow.

A young woman caught her attention, a slender, tall lass with startling brown eyes. It was as if a light was lit behind them. She strutted with confidence, looking at Patience from head to toe.

Patience walked out onto the courtyard inviting the young woman for a quiet chat.

'You are here, to take us away to train us for the Americans, ha?'

Patience was astounded by her forthright tone.

'No, no, why do you think that? I want to take some girls home with me. That is why I'm here.'

'You are not from here, but you don't have an American accent. Where is your home?'

She fired questions without flinching, her determination in wanting to know who Patience was, suggested she had encountered other adoptive parents, prowling around the orphanage, watching them like a prize to be claimed.

'Let's get to know each other's names first. I'm Patience, what's your name?' She knew the girl's name was on the list Balthazar provided, she wanted to hear how the girl introduced herself. Masuyo emphasised the importance of acknowledging names.

'I am Maimoona, I was born in Peshawar. Nice to meet you, sister Patience. You have a good name, like a saint.' She held her head up with regal poise. Her unmistakable suspicion made Patience uncomfortable

'Thank you, I love your name, it suits you, it's full of passion and determination. I admire that quality in a woman.'

'My name means 'trustworthy' in English. I also have to trust before I share who I am, and I can be trusted. I am a very loyal person.'

'Wonderful, you remind me of my sister.'

'You have not told me your country, where are you from?'

'I work here, Maimoona, this is my country, now.'

Patience did not expect the anger spat out at her, she reeled from the fearlessness that emerged from this beautiful, light-eyed lass.

'Liar! I don't know why everybody lies and keeps lying! What am I going to do with the truth? Nobody would believe me anyway! I thought I could trust you, you speak nice words... then you leave, you forget us... they all do it...'

'I'm so sorry to make you feel this way. Who is 'they?'' Under no circumstances could Patience share her identity. Once recruited and safely ensconced at Akbar's Well Centre, then she could divulge more about herself. Maimoona was a curious young woman, her lack of trust in others heightened her need to know more about the people around her. Her life circumstances made her wary of strangers.

'I don't want to talk about it, it makes me sad.' Her anger faded, she looked the picture of a forlorn little girl, unsure, rubbing her feet in the dry dust.

Patience had to move on, she wanted to reassure Maimoona, but knew, she was powerless to make such a claim.

'It was lovely meeting you, Maimoona. I will be back soon.'

She stood facing Patience, her pose suddenly erect again, halting Patience from walking away.

'Take me, please, I will be no trouble, I will do any work, *inshallah*. I can cook, clean, work in the garden, I can fix trucks too. I watched my father do repairs, I used to help him... before... they, the rebels raided our home. Please take me with you.'

This fluctuation from fearless to pitiful to begging, made Patience realise that fearlessness was her defence mechanism.

'You are lucky to be alive, Maimoona, you have great courage.'

'Yes, I hid in the secluded place my father created, under the house — I lay there while they raided my home.'

Patience looked at her, wishing she could walk out with her, to a better life.

'Will you take me?'

'I would love to do that, but paperwork has to be completed, this will take some time. If it's not done the right way, we both will be in a lot of trouble, and might face death.'

'I don't care, dead or alive, nobody knows me. Nobody wants me.'

She did not have the heart to tell Maimoona, that once she was recruited, there might be another woman guiding her through the training.

With the girls' names in place, she left Karachi, the schools, Balthazar, the orphanage and Maimoona, for the long drive back to Akbar's home.

Akbar's driver who was silent on the way to Karachi, struck up a conversation with her, later that night. He observed her through the rear-view mirror, she was deep in thought, troubled.

'You Muslim, sister?' He asked with a searching look at her face in the rear-view mirror, breaking the silence.

She felt uncomfortable, unsure how she should respond to the question — Akbar had not prepared her for this. He assured her that Iqbal was an honest man who would transport her safely to and from Karachi. He cautioned her that Iqbal was a man of few words, that she should not be offended by his lack of acknowledgement of her.

'Why do you ask sir?' She tried not to sound concerned.

'You are so dedicated, you take very good care of the girls like their own mother would. Akbar baba has great respect for you, sister.'

Hearing his warmth and humility, made her instantly relax, she felt drawn to his quiet acknowledgement.

'You are very kind to say so, I guess I must be in my heart then.'

Iqbal smiled, she could see the rising of his glistening, pink cheeks from where she sat in the rear seat. He nodded.

'May Allah always protect you in the work you do. We need more people like you, like mothers.'

He was silent for the rest of the drive.

Patience felt a surge of emotion again, this time with immense gratitude that she was indeed doing what her heart desired.

She contemplated her own spirituality, she was born a Zulu, grew up in a home that did not adhere to an organised religion, yet she learned passion, humility, and selfless service from Varuna. Her mother, Elsie, did not return to the church after her father was murdered. The suspicion that someone within the congregation was responsible, hurt her and left her fearful. Varuna and Elsie united in grief, creating their own haven for their daughters.

Being a good person, was as innate as the pangs of an empty stomach.

The drive was long after an emotionally draining day. The car chugged through mountainous terrain, winding roads, and rough surfaces as a rising chill surrounded them. Her contentment carried her through the night.

SHE ARRIVED at Akbar's home as the sun rose to another frosty morning. Akbar's daughters were collecting eggs from the hen house She could hear the familiar clucking of hens when human company was around. Akbar met her on the verandah.

'Good to see you back, did everything go well, sister?'

'Yes, thank you, it did. I have a few names for you and one, in particular, that I would like to discuss.'

A pot of steaming coffee and two cardamum biscuits left silently by Akbar's smiling wife were welcome. He sat in the seat across the table from her, unable to conceal his earnest expression.

'Sister, I have some news.'

Her ears pricked up, she looked at him, trying to read his thoughts.

'What is it, has something happened to one of the girls while I was away today?'

'They missed you today, but they are well. I received a message from the mission this afternoon, they want you to return home.'

'I was not expecting to hear that! I thought I had a few more weeks here. Why the sudden change?'

'There's a specific reason for the request. They want you to take two of the older girls, that is, escort them to England where a mission agent will be waiting for them for the next round of training.'

This unexpected addition to the plans shook her, she was at the will of the mission's commands.

'How soon do I leave, brother?'

She felt a strange sadness, she was not ready to leave yet. There was so much more she wanted to do here.

He looked at her from above his spectacles, the line across his nose deepened.

'Tomorrow.'

'Tomorrow? Do I get to say goodbye to Azmil and the girls?'

'No, I'm afraid not, mission policy is that you leave as quietly as possible. You understand the girls have formed an emotional connection with you, we have to avoid any sort of detection. The transition with the hand over to the new person should be smooth.'

'I do understand. What about the other eight girls, once the new girls come to the Well Centre?'

'They have been placed, four will remain within Pakistan, and four will be spread around the United States. I will be taking them to Washington, the day after you leave.'

Patience looked at Akbar in disbelief. How long did he know this? Why did he conceal this from her?

'It's all arranged, the other four young women leave later tomorrow, someone from the mission will meet them here and take them to the destinations arranged for them. A week later the new group will arrive, just as they did when you got here. It works like clockwork, you see.'

'Am I allowed to keep in touch with you, to know how they go?'

'I would like that, but I cannot promise it, it's not up to me as you know. The mission has high regard for you. I was given a run-down on you, and I concur dear sister, we have been lucky indeed, to have you here with us. I wish you could stay longer, but who knows, *inshallah*, you might be back.'

Akbar left her to digest this sudden news. She had to leave a message for Azmil and the girls, she could not walk away without saying what she wanted to say. Then there was Maimoona, Akbar must to be convinced that she should be recruited. Balthazar might have more clout than she did. She was relieved that they both agreed that Maimoona was to leave as soon as possible, once Akbar got the go ahead from the mission.

Deep down she knew she would connect with Maimoona again, somewhere in life, somehow…

She drafted a letter to Azmil.

Dear Brother,

It has come as a surprise that I have been asked to leave tomorrow as you might already know. I want to offer my thanks for making me feel like I belonged here, and for sharing your story with me. Thank you for the sacrifice you make to educate young women to make a difference in the world of now and our tomorrows. Please pass on my salaams to them, and tell them I will be looking out for them, wherever they might be.I am leaving my telephone number. If you are ever in Australia, please know you have a home.

Blessings always. Patience.

WRITING the note made her restless, she felt at home here, a part of her soul was being left behind, but Australia was calling. Grace needed her as much as Virginia and the ladies at her Sisters Helping Sisters Organisation. Her family had grown, she had many places she could call home.

She toyed with the idea of calling Grace when she arrived in London and enjoyed thinking about the thrill of the look on her sister's face when she arrived at her door, unannounced.

That element of surprise was the moment she cherished. Childhood joys resurfaced when thoughts of home were close.

She would be homeward bound in a few days, to a known, familiar destination, the first place that was really home.

Optimism is the faith that leads to achievement
~ Helen Keller
(1880 — 1968)

Will a mother and her two daughters escape the trauma of their past lives in a new country?

Will justice be served? Who is maligned, who will be vindicated?

Will she find her creative muse in a villa beside an olive grove?

From a valley in Africa to the Cotswolds in England, heart-warming and gut-wrenching stories on life's challenges and celebrations.

www.ingramcontent.com/pod-product-compliance
Lightning Source LLC
Chambersburg PA
CBHW030638110726
47901CB00002B/492